# THE XANADU PROGRAM

When a body is discovered late one night on a wintry stretch of moorland, the police are unable to establish either the man's identity or the cause of death — until the pathologist suspects murder. It looks like a case that cannot be solved until Mark McNamara returns to his beautiful, estranged wife Louise. A sequence of near-fatal accidents that suddenly befall her lead the curious detectives to resume their investigation, which puts them on the trail of the missing Xanadu Program.

RICHARD CARROLL

◆

# THE XANADU PROGRAM

# LINFORD
*Leicester*

First published in Great Britain in 1983 by
Robert Hale Limited
London

First Linford Edition
published 2002
by arrangement with
Robert Hale Limited
London

British Library CIP Data

Carroll, Richard
　　The Xanadu program.—Large print ed.—
　　Linford mystery library
　　1. Detective and mystery stories
　　2. Large type books
　　I. Title
　　823.9'14 [F]

ISBN 0–7089–9905–0

Published by
F. A. Thorpe (Publishing)
Anstey, Leicestershire

Set by Words & Graphics Ltd.
Anstey, Leicestershire
Printed and bound in Great Britain by
T. J. International Ltd., Padstow, Cornwall

This book is printed on acid-free paper

# 1

The body was discovered on the fourteenth of October. It was found by a young couple making a romantic detour across the heath late on the Friday night. Fortunately, since they were both quite young and neither had previously had close contact with a corpse, they did not examine the body closely but assumed that the man was probably a drunken tramp sleeping it off and gave the prostrate form a wide berth. However, thinking the matter over it occurred to them that it was a cold night and the heath exposed to the biting east wind, and returning to the warm glow of the street-lamps they pondered over the man's predicament. If he were indeed dead drunk the cold might not wake him and he could die of exposure. The young couple worried over him as they walked along the road, wondering whether to take some action although loth to go back and disturb him. Eventually they hailed a passing police patrol car and mentioned the matter to the two officers on duty, giving directions as to where to find him.

The officers duly left their car and walked across the heath to investigate. When they found the man he was not only cold but stiff. He had been dead for some time.

The body was taken to Ravenhill mortuary and the local C.I.D. commenced their routine investigation.

There was no mark on the body to suggest an attack or scuffle, nor any wound which might have caused his unexpected demise. The man appeared to be in his forties or early fifties. His hair was greying. Probable heart attack was the strongest likelihood.

There were, however, strange characteristics about the body which aroused the interest of the investigating officers. His clothes for instance.

The man was impeccably dressed. Dark suit, smart white shirt, tasteful silk tie, quality overcoat, hand-stitched Italian shoes — not, puzzled the local D.I. the sort of gear a man would wear for a late-night stroll across a windy heath. The ground was hardened by a sharp frost. It was very stony and he had not kept to the one well-trodden path but had wandered into the bracken and gorse. His shoes were scuffed and scratched in several places. A man who could afford to ruin shoes like that must be made of money. Furthermore his pockets were quite empty. No money, no car-keys, no papers, not even a pocket handkerchief. There was nothing to identify him.

A search was duly made of the area where he was found in case he had for some reason emptied his pockets and flung his possessions away deliberately but nothing was found. D.I. Williams scratched his head.

The autopsy revealed that the man had been in perfect health up to the time of his death — no infection, no weak organs, no injuries. Extensive inquiries revealed that no one in the area knew him, or had seen him in the vicinity on the fourteenth of October. He was a complete blank.

★ ★ ★

The telephone rang in the local police station. Inspector Williams picked up the receiver. It was the pathologist.

'Inspector Williams? Dr. Highfield here. About your case — the unknown warrior. I think I've established the cause of death.'

Chris Williams whistled with delight. A lead at last. 'I'll be right over,' he said cheerfully and reached for his coat.

Dr. Highfield had called him from his home, a fine white house on the outskirts of the town. As the inspector's car swept into the gravel drive he saw him from the window and opened the door before his visitor could knock.

'Come in,' he said ushering him into his immaculate sitting room.

Inspector Williams felt a little uncomfortable amid the antique splendour of the dark polished furniture and gleaming silver. It was a room to impress rather than express. The pathologist himself seemed out of place in it, an untidy little man in an old tweed jacket, forever threading his fingers through his hair as if he were nervous. The inspector presumed that Mrs. Highfield was responsible for the outward signs of social success. He sat gingerly on the edge of a chair when bidden.

'Well doctor?' he asked eagerly, rubbing his hands together 'What have you got for me?'

Dr. Highfield frowned and picked up his notes from the desk, tugging more frantically at his spare locks than usual.

'It's very strange,' he remarked oddly, putting on his half-moon glasses the better for to read his own spidery writing. 'Very strange indeed. I've not come across another case like it in all my thirty years in this business. No wonder it's taken me so long to come up with the answer.'

Inspector Williams nodded. Dr. Highfield handed him a copy of the report. 'What we have here,' he commented, 'is a man in the prime of his life who suddenly dies without cause. He was not ill. He had no apparent weakness. He was not, as far as we can tell at first glance, attacked in any way.'

'Well then?'

'A man does not just die,' went on the doctor reflectively. 'There has to be some cause of death. I had tried all the obvious possibilities with no results so I tried looking for something obscure.'

'And?'

'And I found it.' The doctor beamed. The inspector grinned. Professional pride was evidently at stake here. Dr. Highfield was a remarkably tenacious individual. Once an idea had taken hold of him he did not easily let go. He had never yet been unable to establish a cause of death and it was a record he intended to keep.

'Congratulations,' offered the policeman. 'What's the damage then?'

'You are going to find this difficult to believe,' warned the doctor, 'but he was poisoned.'

'Poisoned? Accidentally?'

'Hardly. Nor do I think it was suicide. It's a very rare, very deadly poison that kills not only quickly but without leaving any outward trace. No puffiness, no contortions. Hardly any sign at all. Only a slight fever like the onset of a cold.'

'Wouldn't it show up in the stomach?' asked Williams intelligently. 'You examined the contents I take it?'

'It wasn't administered orally,' replied the pathologist. 'I stumbled on the answer by accident. I remembered reading about a similar case in the newspapers some time ago, equally baffling at the time. It seemed a slender chance that the two might be connected but I thought it was worth a try.'

The inspector looked up from the report he was carefully scanning while lending half an ear to his discourse.

'The only external mark I found on the body,' Dr. Highfield went on, 'was a small contusion on the left thigh accompanied by a light scratch. I concluded that the man, whoever he was, must have bumped into something — say the corner of the table — it was about the right height for that, but then, thinking it over I thought about the scratch. A bruise *and* a scratch, you see? He had bumped into something with a sharp edge.'

Inspector Williams nodded to show he was following. 'That's not so surprising

7

surely?' he queried.

'Ah,' went on the doctor, 'that is exactly what made me suspicious. It's not at all surprising. Not something one would normally notice but the man is dead and he has no other wound on him.'

'What's your theory then?'

'You won't believe this,' sighed Dr. Highfield, 'but I feel it's my bounden duty to tell you my conclusions. It is possible that whoever wished to administer the poison might smear it on something sharp, attached to a briefcase say or the point of an umbrella, then bump into the victim as if by accident causing the scratch and the bruise at the same time. The victim would be totally unaware of his danger.'

D.I. Williams wrinkled his nose and thought about it. 'Sounds a bit far-fetched.'

Dr. Highfield scratched his chin. 'So would I think so,' he agreed, 'if I could find any other cause of death but we have a remarkably healthy specimen here. This man had no physical weakness of any kind. He was in excellent health, very fit,

A1, up to the time of his death. A sportsman, I shouldn't wonder, judging from his muscular development. Something caused his untimely demise and according to my tests that something was poison. He didn't drink it or eat it. There was no trace in the stomach or alimentary canal only in the blood. I wouldn't have thought of it if I hadn't remembered this other case.'

Dr. Highfield pushed his spectacles up to the bridge of his nose and pursed his lips. 'The thing is,' he said cautiously, 'in this other case, as I remember, the victim was involved in espionage.'

Inspector Williams looked incredulous. 'A spy? Here?'

Dr. Highfield shrugged. 'It's a very rare poison and extremely difficult to get hold of. Not something your average murderer would get his hands on. You can't buy it in Boots.'

'Even so,' objected the policeman sceptically, subsiding when he saw he was in earnest. 'What would a spy be doing in Ravenhill?'

'Ah, now there you have me,' Dr.

Highfield admitted with a rueful grin. 'Not the strategic centre of the Western world, is it? Still, this espionage is a very mysterious business so everyone keeps telling us. If I'm right it explains why someone is anxious to make it difficult for us to identify the body.'

Inspector Williams stood up. 'Well,' he said thoughtfully, 'if your hunch is right this is not one for your local bobby.'

'That's what I thought,' agreed the doctor. 'I don't want to seem over-fanciful but I don't think we should publish the results of my tests until we've referred the matter higher up. Just in case. I've asked for the inquest to be delayed. That's why I wanted to discuss it with you personally.'

The inspector nodded. 'Thanks,' he acknowledged. 'We don't want to step on anyone's bunions. Well . . . I can't see any holes in your argument. It just seems unlikely.'

'But not impossible.'

'Exactly. Not impossible. And we have nothing better to offer by way of explanation. We'll stamp this one pending and pass it on. See what happens.'

Dr. Highfield grinned and ran his fingers through his hair. 'I'm glad you don't think I'm a head case. I was wondering myself if I wasn't going a bit over the top, but it's a bit of a mystery this one, eh, Chris?'

'It is that,' replied the bemused policeman. 'Bit of a mystery all round.'

# 2

Mark McNamara stood on top of the hill and looked down into the narrow dale. Grey roofs huddled together, the dark stone of the houses seemingly grafted on to the hillsides. Faint puffs of smoke spiralled from some of the chimneys. White washing flapped in the strong breeze. It was a beautiful autumn day, the blue sky veined with traces of white cloud like a lace agate. The sun shone coldly but with a sharp brilliance that intensified the gold and bronze of the crackling bracken, the copper of the burnished leaves that fluttered from the distant trees. Autumn was his favourite time of year, a time of dark fire and deep burning. Autumn reminded him of old passions rekindled, buried hopes stirring — the slow, sultry glow of an affair mellowed by experience. Spring was for young lovers. Give him autumn any day. Some of the trees were already naked reaching long withered fingers towards the sky. There was a stark reality about the landscape, no illusions, no escape. Mark stuck his hands in his pockets and ambled along the uneven path. It was a long way down.

He exchanged friendly nods with a couple of lads jumping on and off a hollow log with the undirected restlessness of youth. They were a couple of cheeky lads, one dark, one red-haired, with the ebullient confidence of those who know they are bound to get into mischief so why worry.

'Hey, mister,' said one of the lads, 'You dunna want to go down there.'

Mark had been about to take a short cut across the heath. He paused on the path.

'Why not?'

'That's where they found the body,' relished the red-haired boy with a touch of ghoulish glee. 'All covered with blood. Horrible it were.'

Mark raised his eyebrows. 'Funny, I heard the man died of a heart attack,' he responded coolly.

The boys looked crestfallen. His adult

calm spoilt their delight in the thrill of fear.

'That's what they *said*,' protested the dark-haired lad, 'but we think he were murdered. They had all sorts of police up here. Dozens of them. Dogs an' all. Why would they have dogs if it were just a heart attack?'

Mark pursed his lips thoughtfully. 'Why indeed,' he agreed.

'We can show you exactly where he were found,' volunteered the red-head eagerly. 'Want to see?'

Mark considered his offer then nodded cheerfully, infected by their excitement. 'Why not? Lead the way.'

Delighted to have someone to share their enthusiasm for the adventure the two boys slid off the log and struck out across the heath with Mark strolling languidly in their wake. They reached the spot long before he did and stood fretfully scuffling the grass, impatiently waving him on.

'Here it is,' proclaimed the dark boy, as Mark came up to them. 'You can see where the bracken's been flattened.

That's where he were lying.'

'No blood though,' added his companion, a shade disappointed, 'They must've cleaned it all up.'

Mark smiled. 'You're sure you've got the right place?'

Both boys nodded emphatically. 'He were found in the dead of night by Andy James and our Janice. They practically fell over him,' volunteered the redhead.

Mark feigned decent astonishment.

'What were they doing here at the dead of night?' he asked reasonably.

The boy pulled a face and looked slightly embarassed.

'They're courting,' he said sheepishly, scuffling his foot from side to side, evidently considering this an unfit subject for manly conversation.

Mark nodded, understanding.

'I wonder what he was doing here?' he mused aloud.

The boy shrugged. 'No one knows. They dunna even know his name yet. They've got to check his teeth.'

'His teeth?'

The red-haired lad observed Mark

gravely as a man of experience might regard a novice. 'They can tell who you are from your teeth,' he explained. 'No two sets of teeth are alike. My uncle Bob told me that. He's a copper.'

'I thought that was fingerprints.'

'Teeth as well.'

Mark accepted his words of wisdom. 'Fancy that. Teeth. Well . . . ' he added thoughtfully, 'we'll just have to hope they're his own.'

The boys kicked around the bracken for a bit searching for clues but finding none they quickly grew tired of the subject and bidding Mark an abrupt farewell allowed their restless energy to carry them in the direction of the park where conker trees abounded and big sticks to throw up into the branches. Mark watched them go racing each other down the hill out of sheer exuberance of spirit. He smiled a trifle wistfully. Boys will be boys.

He stood for a moment staring down at the spot where the dead man had lain then looked up and around him. Where would he have been going at that time of night? He had left the path so obviously he was not intending to take the usual route into the town.

Standing in the dead man's place Mark surveyed the scene. If he had been intending to go into Ravenhill he was going a long way round. He was cutting across the heath roughly parallel with the line of the High Street some few hundred feet below. Which way was he facing when he fell? One direction took him back up the hill. If he followed that line he would eventually reach the moors. Not the place for a stranger on a cold October night, he reflected. Back to the path? Why leave it in the first place? Mark turned himself around. Ahead, slightly below him, stood a row of tiny houses, their back gardens facing the windy heath and stoutly protected by high walls. Mark stood and surveyed them for a moment or two, then lining himself up carefully with the position of the fallen body as indicated by the flattened bracken he set out in a direct line.

He reached the back of one of the centre-terrace houses. The back gate was green. It needed painting. He gingerly lifted the latch and went in.

The backyard was untidy, littered with crates and old furniture. A dustbin stood without its lid as if it had just been emptied. A line of washing hung from the kitchen door to the roof of the outside lavatory. Mark surveyed the laundry, all female clothing — a row of knickers pegged out like a signal to the fleet.

'A naval signal,' he murmured mildly to himself, 'England expects . . . '

He fingered a long black lace night-dress. It was barely wet. The kitchen door opened and a woman came out. She was carrying a laundry basket evidently to fetch the clothes in. Seeing him standing there she halted suddenly and stared.

He stared back. She was slightly built and wearing jeans which emphasised the curve of her hips. A clinging black jumper did nothing to disguise the swell of her full round breasts. Her hair was extraordinary, a dark red, neither ginger nor auburn but a deep fiery colour finely touched with gold. It fell to her shoulders and a long fringe partly veiled her eyes but he could not help noticing them. They were the dark blue of lapis lazuli and at this moment they were burning.

'What the hell do you want?' she snapped angrily.

He started to laugh. 'Of all the bars in all the towns and I had to pick this one,' he said cheerfully.

Her expression of angry amazement turned to disgust. 'Not Casablanca.'

'Sorry. Don't you like that one? Hello then.'

'Hello.'

They stood looking at each other for a minute like prize fighters weighing each other up.

'Aren't you going to ask me in?' he said at last.

She thrust the laundry basket into his arms. 'Hold that. You might as well make yourself useful.'

Briskly she began to unpeg the clothes, folding them hurriedly and dropping them into the basket as she went along. Obediently he followed her along the line.

'I like that,' he said pointing to the nightdress.

'Not for your benefit,' she snapped, folding it quickly and throwing it on the pile.

'Whose then?'

'Mind your own business.'

The last of the clothes collected she took the basket off him and sailed into the house. He followed her. She made no attempt to stop him.

In the kitchen all was tidy in contrast to the muddle of the garden. She placed the basket on the table and began to refold the washing properly. He sat down.

'When did you move here?'

'After you left.'

He looked round approvingly. 'Very nice.'

'I think so.' She paused in her chore. 'It's my half of the money from the sale of the house. Yours is in the bank.'

He shrugged. 'You didn't have to stint yourself.'

She glanced at him ruefully then turned away. 'This'll do me.'

She went through into the lounge. He followed her, tagging on like a faithful puppy. She went to a desk and rifled through the top drawer.

'I've got it all here. I've kept a proper record. I was going to send it to you when I found out where you'd gone.'

He stood behind her stroking her hair. She pulled away angrily and turned to face him, her eyes blazing with anger.

'Why the hell did you come?' she demanded bluntly.

He raised his eyebrows slightly and started to unbutton his shirt.

'I've come to claim my rights,' he said arrogantly.

She snorted derisively. 'What rights?'

He grinned wickedly and folded her tightly in his arms.

'Conjugal rights.'

# 3

Inspector Williams stuck his hands in his pockets and bowed his head before the gusting wind. The icy river swirled under the bridge swollen by the streams pouring down from the high ground. The old sign creaked over the 'Dog and Muffler' as he approached across the street.

A man was standing outside waiting for him. He was a stocky, heavily-built man enveloped in a large, navy overcoat. His hair was thinning. A few ginger wisps clung to the crown of his head brushed forward to appease his vanity. His eyebrows were thick and bushy. His eyes were pale, blue, vague and misty as if his mind was permanently wandering. He had big feet which he kept stamping up and down, either cold or impatient. You could tell he was a policeman.

Inspector Williams hailed him. 'You must be Sergeant . . . ?'

'Knutter sir, with a K.'

The inspector laughed. 'That's right. Good name for a copper.'

Sergeant Knutter considered it thoughtfully. 'It has occasioned the odd ribald comment in the past, sir, but I've learned to live with it.'

'Well, Sergeant Knutter. You've been sent to join me, I believe.'

'Sent to join your team, sir.'

'I am my team.'

'In that case, sir, I am, so to speak, the cavalry. My instructions are to assist you in your inquiries with regard to the missing person.'

'He's not missing,' objected the inspector. 'We've found him all right. Dead as a doornail. I doubt if he'll be going anywhere now.'

'I hope not sir.'

The sergeant smiled faintly, a reluctant, thin-lipped smile as if he hardly dared laugh at his own jokes.

'You don't know who he is yet?' he went on.

'No.'

'Or how he came to be in Ravenhill?'

'No.'

'Not much to go on.'

'Nothing at all.'

Knutter shrugged. 'Then it would seem that this case is wide open, sir.'

'As a barn door,' Williams agreed cordially.

Knutter smiled, more engagingly this time. He had surprising charm for a man apparently constructed out of granite which was disconcertingly disarming.

'Then I suggest, sir, we betake ourselves to this hostelry and inquire after the maitre d. if he has two pints of the county's finest, then we can make ourselves comfortable and indulge in a little quiet contemplation. There is not a question in the world which cannot be answered by philosophy.'

Inspector Williams shivered and glanced through the pub window at the inviting scene of comfort and warmth inside the building.

'Good idea,' he assented and motioned Knutter to lead the way.

The two policemen were just about to enter the lounge bar when two young lads came hurtling out. They stopped them in their tracks.

'Have you been in there?' demanded the young inspector sternly.

'Only bringing back the empties,' claimed one lad innocently.

'You're not supposed to go in there,' Williams lectured him solemnly 'You know that. These are licensed premises. You're under age. If I catch you here again you'll be for it. I'll see your dad gets to know about it.'

The lad shrugged insolently. 'Me dad knows already. It were him what sent us.'

The two policemen exchanged glances and raised their eyes heavenward.

'Go on. Hop it,' said the inspector, jerking his thumb down the street, 'and remember what I said.'

\* \* \*

The boys nodded and dashed away, dodging out of sight in no time.

Williams sighed. 'I don't know,' he said. 'What do you do? You can't blame the kids if their parents don't teach them right from wrong. Can your philosophy

25

answer that one?'

Sergeant Knutter raised his finger. 'If there is righteousness in the heart, there will be beauty in the character. If there be beauty in the character there will be harmony in the home. If there be harmony in the home there will be order in the nation. When there is order in the nation there will be peace in the world,' he declaimed, 'Chinese proverb. Until that time we'll never be out of a job.'

He laughed suddenly, an abrupt explosion like a car-exhaust back-firing, and led the inspector into the pub.

'I'm told,' said Williams, as they reached the bar, '. . . two pints of best Bill . . . that you're a bit of a maverick, Sergeant.'

Sergeant Knutter smiled engagingly and a brilliant point of fire lit his pale blue eyes.

'Not me, sir,' he said genially. 'I think you'll find I'm as gentle as a lamb.'

★ ★ ★

Mark rolled over in bed as his mind slopped into consciousness. He had been floating in a sea of pleasant dreams. He opened his eyes. His wife was sitting beside him wrapped in the top sheet.

'I fell asleep,' he said unnecessarily.

'I noticed,' she said. 'You always do.'

He ran his fingers up the ridge of her spine making her shudder involuntarily.

'Don't do that.'

'Have you missed me?'

She looked at him straight. 'What a bloody stupid question.'

The telephone was ringing. They could hear its persistent buzz-buzz through the walls. She pulled herself out of bed and went to answer it, trailing the end of the sheet behind her.

Mark got up and reached for his trousers. She had left the bedroom door open. As he was climbing into them he could hear snatches of her conversation.

'No,' she was saying urgently, 'don't come. It's not convenient. I've got someone here.'

The caller was evidently protesting because she repeated her message several times.

Mark dressed and followed her down

the stairs. She put the phone down as he reached the bottom step. He raised his eyebrows.

'Boyfriend?' he inquired. 'I hope I'm not spoiling anything.'

'Mind your own bloody business,' she snapped.

'I thought it was my business,' he said sarcastically, 'or am I not supposed to mind who my wife is running around with?'

'I'm not running around,' she retorted hotly. 'He's a friend. All right? Just a friend.'

He hunched his shoulders dismissively. 'If it's none of my business . . . ' She threw a directory at him. It struck him squarely but without much force.

'You've got a bloody cheek,' she cried painfully. 'You disappeared twelve months ago. Walked out and left me without a word of explanation, just a note on the mantelpiece saying you'd be in touch. I haven't heard a word from you since. Not a letter. Not one phone-call. Did you honestly expect to come walking in here cool as you please and find nothing had changed? What the hell do you think I am?'

Her eyes met his blazing with fury, hurt pride and righteous indignation. He met her gaze coolly for a moment then guilt flooded over him and he found himself forced to look away.

'Not faithful,' he said cruelly and went into the kitchen to make himself a cup of coffee.

'You bastard!' she screamed, and he heard the door slam behind him.

The kettle took ages to boil. By the time it was whistling she had joined him again, fully dressed now.

'Do you want one?' he pointed to the waiting coffee mugs.

She nodded. 'Why?'

'Why what?'

'Why did you come back?'

The abruptness of her question made him laugh. Same old Lou, no beating about the bush. 'Accident.'

'Accident?'

He poured the water on to the coffee and stirred it thoughtfully. 'I didn't know you lived here. I'm on business. I heard about the body — you know the one they found on the heath behind here. I was just snooping around. Unfortunate coincidence.'

'Very unfortunate.' She tried to keep the disappointment out of her voice but it still came out a bit raw.

'I didn't mean it like that.' He kissed her on the cheek, a sign that the quarrel was over. He handed her the mug and she settled herself on one of the stools. He leaned against the doorpost. For a moment there was no sound except the scraping of the spoon in his coffee cup.

'Why did you go?' she asked quietly, keeping very calm now. 'Why did you just walk out like that? You don't have to make excuses, I just want to know. What did I do wrong?'

He sighed. It was a question he had been hoping to avoid. 'It wasn't you,' he said at last rather lamely 'You didn't do anything.'

'What then?'

'It was everything. The job, the mortgage, marriage . . . living up to other people's expectations, the future all mapped out before us — daren't put a bloody foot wrong or you slip right back to the bottom of the pile. I'm just irresponsible. Immature if you like. I just couldn't stick it.'

'That's why you became a journalist? For an irregular life?'

'It was just a chance that came up.'

'You didn't have to walk out.'

'I had to get away. I was cracking up.'

'You could have told me. We could have worked something out. I'd have helped you.'

He frowned as if the whole discussion were distasteful to him. 'I don't think anyone could help. Not even a psychiatrist. It was just something I had to sort out for myself. A clean break seemed the best idea. I'm sorry.'

'Is that all you've got to say? Sorry.'

'Yes.'

She looked down into her coffee and sipped it slowly. 'That's it then.'

'Yes.'

He put down his coffee and went to sit beside her. He touched her hair gently. 'I'm sorry, Lou. I really am. I'd try to

31

explain — I tried to write but the words wouldn't come right. Whenever I try to talk about things that really matter I just find myself drowning in cliches. None of it means anything. It's not that I don't love you.'

She stuck out her lower lip in a sulky expression. 'I find that hard to believe.'

He sighed and let his hand fall from her shoulder. 'I suppose you do. Of course you do. I'm just sorry, that's all.'

She smoothed her hair self-consciously. 'I suppose that's something anyway. Now you're here we can work something out. We'll have to do something, split the furniture and everything.'

'You can have it.'

He looked away and stared out of the window evidently reluctant to talk about it.

'Well,' she said matter-of-factly, 'What *are* you doing in Ravenhill if you haven't come to see me?'

'It's just research, that's all. Two nations — how the rich are getting rich and the poor are getting poorer, that sort of thing.'

'How the other half live?'

'That's it.'

'I suppose we're the other half.'

He grinned. 'I'm afraid so.'

She wrinkled her nose. 'Where does the body come in?'

'Nowhere. I was just curious.'

'Journalist's instinct?'

'Something like that.'

He hesitated, then said suddenly. 'Lou, can I stay here?'

She looked up a trifle startled. 'Stay?'

'I'll be here for a while on this assignment. There's not much accommodation in Ravenhill. I've got nowhere to stay as yet.'

'Of course you can stay,' her face darkened angrily, 'this is your home.'

His expression softened slightly. He touched her cheek so she would raise her eyes to meet his. They were dark as lapis lazuli burning with deep fire and the lashes were wet with tears.

'Still?'

She swallowed and said defiantly, 'You're still my husband. We're not divorced. Yet.'

She looked away abruptly and stood up, pushing him aside. She rinsed the mugs under the tap and put them away.

'Well?' she demanded, tying on an apron and masking her uncertainty with a show of efficiency, 'If you're staying you'd better tell me what you want for dinner.'

# 4

The papers on the case of the poisoned man had been passed on to a higher authority for inspection. They came back with the instruction 'Proceed as usual'. The case was to be treated as murder. Dental records revealed nothing of the man's identity. He had apparently never had dental treatment. Another blank.

'What does that suggest to you?' Inspector Williams asked his sergeant, fishing for ideas.

Sergeant Knutter contemplated the problem for a moment. 'Either his mother never let him eat sweeties or he's a foreigner,' he suggested.

'A foreigner?'

'Had his teeth fixed abroad.'

Inspector Williams sat down at his desk and swivelled his chair so that he could put his feet up. 'From where?'

His sergeant perched himself on the window-sill and concentrated his gaze on the deserted car-park. 'From Italy? His shoes were Italian.'

'Everyone wears Italian shoes these days. Not very conclusive proof.' Sergeant Knutter nodded his agreement. 'All we've got to go on.'

Williams sighed. 'I suppose you're right. Let's proceed on the assumption that the man is Italian. We could check with immigration and maybe the Italian Embassy — see if any of their nationals has been reported missing here. Tell you what, Sergeant. You look as if you could do with some exercise. You check on Italian families living in Ravenhill. There can't be that many. He must have been intending to contact someone here right?'

'Seems likely. Not much of a tourist attraction.'

'So, if we assume that he is Italian — or was, I should say — and intended to contact someone here, maybe a relative, that gives us a starting point. Call round the families, show them the picture, see if anyone recognises him.'

'Think it's the Mafia,' inquired Sergeant Knutter flippantly, 'moving in on the Jubilee Street Pizza Parlour?'

Inspector Williams smiled. 'It could be, Sergeant. Just right at this moment I'm prepared to accept any suggestions.'

'How about a drink, sir? It's my shout.'

There was a momentary pause then the two men dived for their coats.

'Now I know why they sent you to me,' observed Chris Williams as he went through the door, 'You're full of bright ideas.'

★  ★  ★

The saloon bar of the 'Dog and Muffler' was packed with bodies. It was warm and stuffy, smoke rising in the already fuggy atmosphere. Mark McNamara elbowed his way through the throng. Outside, the sky was white with threatening snow and a freezing wind chased the fallen leaves along the pavement. His hands were numb with cold. It was good to be inside. Across the room he spotted Inspector Williams and his colleague seated at a corner table. He pushed his way over to them.

'Inspector Williams?'

Inspector Williams looked up. He beheld a tall young man, thirty-fiveish, with curling ginger hair and a frank, open expression. He was a good-looking man, well-dressed in a casual way, a bit trendy for Ravenhill.

'What can I do for you?'

'My name in Mark McNamara. I'm a reporter on the Clarion. Mind if I join you?'

Williams shook his head and motioned to the empty seat. Mark sat down cheerfully.

'My colleague, Frank Tattersall, advised me to get in touch with you.'

Recognition dawned on the policeman's face. 'Yes I know Frank. How is he these days?'

'Tied to a desk mostly. He's an editor now. Misses the thrill of the chase, I think.'

Inspector Williams laughed. 'He would. He was always ahead of most of us. I knew him when I worked with the Met. Great crime reporter Frank. You one of his protéges?'

Mark grinned. 'No such luck.'

'I thought you were investigating the murder,' explained Williams 'What do you want with me?'

'Murder?' an interested reporter looked up, 'I thought it was a heart attack?'

'We think not.'

Mark pondered this for a while then recalled his immediate business. 'Actually that's not what I'm here for. Nothing so interesting. Politics and Economics are my speciality. I'm doing a piece on the effects of the recession in different parts of the country.'

'How can I help you?' The inspector looked puzzled.

'Well, it's a matter of contacts really. I've just arrived in Ravenhill. Don't know a soul. I was hoping you could put me in touch with a few people — people who've got their finger on the pulse of things — trade unionists, local councillors, ecetera. You must know who counts around here.'

'''Tis we, who lost in stormy visions, keep

With phantoms an unprofitable strife,

And in mad trance, strike with our spirit's knife

Invulnerable nothings,'' intoned Sergeant Knutter solemnly.

'Eh?'

'Times are hard. Look to the revolution. The chimera of social change. Not that anything does change. Like the cargo cults — the ship that never comes in although it's always going to. It's a great time for evangelists.'

Williams and Mark looked at him in surprise. Sergeant Knutter regarded them with an expression of bland innocence.

'Just an observation,' he pointed out.

Mark tapped the table with his fingertips. 'Well, that's what I want to know. Who are the evangelists in Ravenhill? Who is the average man going to turn to when the going gets tough? Capitalist or Communist?'

'More likely Methodist,' pointed out Inspector Williams, 'There's a great tradition of that round here.'

'Well, who do I see to find out?' persisted Mark.

Inspector Williams thought for a minute.

'I could put you in touch with Edward Kelsey,' he suggested 'He's the most influential trade unionist round here.'

'*The* Edward Kelsey?' Mark looked up in surprise.

'That's the one. Lynch-pin of the Labour movement. He's been a red in his day, they say. Mellowed a bit now but he's still pretty important. He was born and bred in Ravenhill. They lay a lot of store in what he says round here. Not much to know about the town that he can't tell you. He's also a local councillor *and* a Methodist lay preacher so he can put you in touch with the sort of people you want to meet. I'll give him a ring and see if I can arrange an introduction.'

'Would you do that? Really?'

'Friend of Frank's.'

'Great. Thanks.' Mark beamed. 'Let's drink to that. What'll you have? Can I get you anything to eat? Do they do food in here?'

'Molly's chicken and ham pies are a dream,' Chris Williams informed him.

'Fine. Three then? And same again?'

They nodded and he went to the bar.

Inspector Williams watched him closely as he stood joking with the barmaid. He had the knack of fitting into any company, a gift that would be useful in his trade. He came back with the beer, balancing it precariously on a tray that was too small.

'About this murder,' he remarked, placing the glasses on the table, 'It's not my brief but as a newsman I'm honour bound to take an interest. I might look into it a bit. You won't mind, will you?'

The inspector shook his head and dipped his lips into the creamy head of his beer. 'Anything you can find out,' he said, licking the foam from his lips with relish, 'we'll be glad to hear. If you can come up with the identity of the victim you're a better man than I am, Gunga Din.'

'You don't even know who he is?'

'Not the foggiest. Sergeant Knutter here has a theory that he's Italian based on an examination of his shoes.'

'His shoes?'

'Gucci no less.'

Mark started to laugh. 'What about his vest?'

'Marks and Spencer.'

'No identification?'

'None whatsoever.'

'Well,' Mark placed his glass down on the shiny surface of the table and sat back in his seat, 'there's nothing like a mystery, is there?'

★　★　★

There were a few Italian families in Ravenhill but it did not take Sergeant Knutter long to establish that none of them could identify the dead man. He returned to the station cold, footsore and discontented, having drawn another blank.

'That's it then,' said Inspector Williams as he told him the results of his inquiries 'I guess we'll just have to leave the case open. Another unsolved crime for the statistics.'

Sergeant Knutter looked disappointed. 'I don't like mysteries.'

Williams shrugged helplessly. 'Neither do I, but we seem to have reached a dead end on this one.'

'I'd like to keep poking around a bit, if you don't mind, sir. There may be some connection we've overlooked. I just have a feeling about this one. A funny feeling in my guts.'

'Could be indigestion.'

'Could be. All the same, sir . . . ?'

The young inspector looked at his sturdy sergeant. His brow was creased in concentration. He was the sort of copper who once he got his nose into a case could smell his way through. Man-management, wasn't that what it was all about? Taking a chance on the right people? He handed him the file.

'C Division don't seem to be in a hurry to have you back.'

'No, sir. They're involved in a long stake-out. Hours of observation, sir, sitting in the back of a van with nothing to do but remember how long its been since you last went to the lavatory. I've got a weak bladder, sir.'

Inspector Williams guffawed. 'Point taken. All right then. Carry on, Sergeant. Let me know if you come up with anything.'

Sergeant Knutter grinned appreciatively. 'Another week is all I need.'

'To avoid the stake-out or crack this
case?'

Sergeant Knutter looked pained. 'Both,
sir. Of course.'

★　★　★

The blank character of the dead man
bothered Chris Williams. He was not
happy to have a murder on his patch, still
less to find it was a murder which he
could not solve. He went over and over in
his mind the slender clues that they had
gathered, searching for some missing
piece that might make the jigsaw fit
together and reveal a picture but each
time he was forced to abandon the
problem without getting any further. Like
Sergeant Knutter he disliked mysteries
but what he disliked even more was the
thought that a professional killing had
been dumped on his territory in the
knowledge that hick-detectives would not
be able to unravel the source or purpose
of the crime. He met Dr. Highfield in

court later that week and while they were sitting outside waiting to be called he took the opportunity to question him further.

'If only there was something,' he complained. 'Some little thing that we could use as a starting-point. Our only hunch so far is that he's a foreigner.'

'A foreigner?' Dr. Highfield tugged at his hair distractedly.

'No dental work in this country. But from where? Italian we thought from his shoes but he could have bought those in London.'

Dr. Highfield thought carefully. 'There is the poison,' he suggested.

'What about it?'

'Well, it's not much more of a clue than the shoes really. It's very rare as I mentioned before, not easy to get hold of, but I should have imagined it was acquired through one of the research laboratories for tropical medicine, but assuming it was not, the source of the poison is to be found in Africa.'

'Africa?'

'Unfortunately, over a very wide area.

Central and Southern Africa is about the best I can do. Doesn't narrow it down very much.'

'South African say? The man was white.'

Dr. Highfield wiped his spectacles meditatively. 'It's just a possibility. It could have been acquired from a laboratory anywhere in Europe or America. It's just a suggestion. Something to bear in mind.'

'Thanks very much' Inspector Williams stood up as he heard his name called. 'I will bear it in mind. It's a thought anyway.'

# 5

Mark drove home in a puzzled and distracted frame of mind. He felt it behoved him to take an interest in the murder inquiry. It had all the ingredients of a good story provided the mystery could be solved. At present it would hardly be covered by two lines and a by-line. At all events it promised to hold out more hope for the future of a newly established reporter than his present assignment. He was a good journalist, a talented writer, but no one could imagine that he would make much of a name for himself churning out dreary if well-reasoned articles about the state of the economy. Just this once, he thought, he'd better do what was expected of him.

The economic situation was pretty boring anyway — just going from bad to worse and no one had any idea what to do about it, so what was there to say? The political aspects were not much more interesting. No one particularly wanted to save the world since much of it didn't seem worth saving anyway. Backs to the wall, chaps, tighten your belts and dish out the Dunkirk spirit like cod-liver oil. Any attempt to lighten the darkness was met with a wave of weary cynicism and the feeling that total abstention was better than making any of the choices on offer. Did anyone really believe that the slump was caused by homosexuality and the four-letter word graffiti that passed as art these days or that the solution to any of it was mindless, angry violence? Destruction rather than construction. Inversion rather than perversion. Dunkirk, it was realised, was a bloody disaster and whether you faced it with heroic dignity of buried your head in the sand it came to the same thing — miserable failure. If you fought and won you were wrong. If you fought and lost you were wrong. So why bother to fight at all? Inertia is always the easiest way out.

Driving through the narrow streets of Ravenhill, the rows of grey houses seemingly shadows of each other, Mark looked at the brave new world that seemed to be pedalling backwards. The chimneys had all sprouted complicated television aerials like so many toasting forks pricking the sky. Apart from that very little had changed. Most of the men were out of work. Most of the women were bitter. That was the trouble with brave new worlds — the further you reached the more you had to lose. He thought of his own home that his wife had sold to come and live in this dark little valley. He wondered why she had chosen it. Penance perhaps for her failure as woman and wife, although it had not been her failure but his. That was his own personal Dunkirk. No heroic dignity on his part, he had run like a rabbit without even knowing why. Tactical retreat sounded better but didn't alter the fact. Now he was back. To start again or not to . . . that was the question.

He parked the car a few doors down the road where there was a space and walked up, then remembered that he had no key. He recalled Lou had told him to go round the back where the door was always open, so he dodged down the alleyway between the houses and followed the cobbled path along the back of the terraces. Reaching Lou's green gate he let himself in, opened the back door and looked into the kitchen.

He stood, shocked, on the threshold. Lou was standing in front of him close to another man, his arms encircling her. It was not that fact in itself that shocked him, embarassing though the circumstance was, but the man himself. He was grey, old enough to be her father — not handsome or distinguished — just old.

A sharp pain of jealous rage stabbed through him. He didn't bother to ask himself why. He slammed the door shut behind him to draw their attention.

'Get out,' he said sharply.

Lou looked round and gasped slightly. 'This is my husband,' she said for the benefit of her guest.

'Out,' repeated Mark crisply, and opened the door again.

The man opened his mouth as if he were going to say something, then appeared to think better of it. He shrugged, patted Lou on the backside and walked out past Mark, who stood back tensely to let him pass. He slammed the door shut behind him with such force it shook between its posts.

'Mark,' cried Lou, passionately annoyed and embarassed, 'did you have to?'

He turned to face her. She could see he was furious.

'Did *I* have to?' he raged. 'Did *you* have to? Is he the best you can do? If you're going to have an affair you might at least pick on someone of your own age. I have my pride to think of.'

She frowned and bit her lip, turning away until she could control her temper. 'There's no need to be offensive. He's a friend.'

'I could see that.'

'A friend, Mark. So just forget what you were thinking, all right? He's a lonely man. His wife died. I've been lonely, too. We've got something in common.'

He let out an exasperated sigh and stared at the ceiling. Guilty feelings came flooding back to him again but this time they only fuelled his anger.

'It's my fault again.'

'Yes, it is your fault.' She banged the bread board down hard on the table to relieve her feelings in an act of physical violence. 'I'm not bloody apologising. Why should I? What if he is my lover? What is it to you?'

He shrugged petulantly, not having a good answer. 'Nothing. I just thought you'd have better taste.'

She picked up the board and threw it at him shattering the glass in the window.

'Missed me,' he said aggravatingly.

'No, I didn't,' she said bitterly 'Not one little bit.'

If he was hurt he refused to show it. 'I didn't suppose you would,' he sneered back, 'but you didn't have to accept just any replacement. You should have told me, Lou. If I'd known you were that desperate I'd have come back sooner. I'd have eased your frustration just as a matter of duty.'

She said nothing, just stared at him. Anger and emotion were welling up inside her but the jumble of thoughts and accusations formed no words only a great brittle defensive barrier that was barely strong enough to hold back the flood. He could see the pressure building up in her and waited nervously for the explosion. Suddenly she burst into tears and ran out of the room.

He had gone too far and he knew it. He heard the front door slam and guiltily thought of her running in the street tears streaming down her face. He had no right to talk to her like that and the knowledge made him despise himself. Nothing would be achieved in anger. He had no right to take his own failures out on her. Impulsively making up his mind he went after her, leaving the front door open. She was already half-way down the street but had stopped running. He chased after her.

'Lou! Lou! Wait . . . '

She looked straight ahead and kept on walking. He caught her by the arm forcing her to stop.

'I'm sorry. I didn't mean what I said.'

'Didn't you? It didn't sound like a joke to me.'

Her eyes were full of tears. He hated to see her cry. It was a weak spot in him. He avoided so many unpleasant scenes because he hated to see her cry. He ran away rather than face a row. She had the ability to touch him which frightened him. He liked to think he was always in control of himself, invulnerable. He hated to have his guard penetrated. It made him insecure. He felt insecure now facing her accusing painful glare like a naughty boy who has betrayed his mother's trust in him.

'You know I didn't.' In moments of stress he began to stammer and flounder, remnants of a tongue-tied childhood that followed like a shadow the easy-mannered and readily articulate man. 'It was just . . . I didn't . . . Come home, Lou. We can't talk about it in the street.'

She looked at him squarely. There was something appealing about his vulnerability. Strangely it was not at his most charming and entertaining that she loved him best but when he stood before her as now, a trembling, vulnerable little boy with anxious eyes desperate to please.

Women admire men for their strengths but love them for their weaknesses. Lou was no different from the rest of her sex. She felt a surge of love for him now that she could feel her power over him. The rest of the time she couldn't touch him. No one could.

She began to walk with him slowly back down the street towards the house. 'There was no need to behave like that,' she said strictly. 'Why did you make such a scene?'

He hung his head repentantly. 'I was jealous, I suppose. What do you expect when I find you with another man?'

She stopped suddenly in her tracks and looked up at him with hopeful eyes. 'Were you?'

She was flung into his arms. All they were aware of was an almighty bang and the force of the blast. When they looked round they saw shattered glass falling from the windows and the front door hanging off its hinges. Mark hugged his wife closer to him.

'What in God's name,' he said, 'was that?'

# 6

'Well,' said Inspector Williams, shuffling the papers together and looking over them at the white-faced couple sitting on the other side of his desk, 'it appears that your house, Mrs. McNamara, was damaged by an explosion caused by a small incendiary device — not enough to totally destroy the building but certainly enough to kill anyone on the ground floor.'

Mark whistled.

'A bomb?'

'A bomb.' The young policeman looked from one stunned face to the other. 'Now could either of you tell me why anyone would wish to plant a bomb in your home?'

Mark shook his head. 'No reason that I know of.'

'You haven't been involved in any investigations that might have made you enemies?'

'No. No investigations. Just commentaries. Summaries of economic trends, political implications of changes in the minimum lending rate, that sort of thing. Not exactly scoop material.'

Inspector Williams nodded in agreement. 'Mrs. McNamara?'

Lou shook her head.

'Who has access to your house? Someone must have planted the device.'

'The postman.'

'Pardon?'

She passed a hand across her brow flicking her fringe out of her eyes. 'I should've thought ... A package was delivered. Right address but wrong name. I didn't think anything of it. No reason why I should. I didn't open it. I was going to re-post it — Return to Sender. It was on the coffee table.'

'Thank God you didn't open it,' Mark squeezed her hand comfortingly. She looked drawn and tired, defeated.

'Perhaps it was not intended that you should,' mused Williams thoughtfully. 'Right address but wrong name. Naturally you would assume it was for someone else. What was the name, Mrs. McNamara? Can you remember?'

Lou thought for a minute then shook her head. 'I didn't really notice.'

Inspector Williams nodded sympathetically and offered her a cigarette. She tried to light it but couldn't hold it steady. Mark lit it for her.

'Well, we have two possibilities,' said the policeman, 'either someone wishes to harm — or at least frighten — one or both of you, or the parcel was wrongly addressed and was intended for someone else, the name on the label whatever it was.'

'Is that likely?' objected Mark. 'It would have to be someone in Ravenhill. They couldn't have got the whole address wrong surely? Unless it was meant for one of the neighbours.'

'That,' pointed out the inspector, 'is something we shall have to look into. Otherwise . . . '

'Another mystery?'

The inspector shuffled his papers and put them back in the file. 'Yes,' he agreed with a perplexed frown, 'another mystery.'

Sergeant Knutter walked briskly across the wind-blown heath. The heather and gorse rippled like the surface of an inland sea, whipped by the breeze that chased the wild clouds across the sky. It was a sharp day — sharp wind, penetrating cold — sharp colours, brilliant primary blues and greens, bright yellow. Sergeant Knutter inhaled with satisfaction. It felt a good day to be alive.

He spotted the two young lads he had encountered in the doorway of 'The Dog and Muffler' with Inspector Williams. They were chasing each other round, whirling in the wind, arms outstretched in imitation of the spiralling seed-blades of the sycamore. He walked up to them casually.

They halted when they saw him as if anxious that he would scold them for some crime as yet uncommitted or undetected but he smiled genially and their faces relaxed.

'You investigating the murder?' one hailed him cheerfully, his red curls tousled by the breeze.

He nodded in a friendly manner. He had a way with kids.

'Re-visiting the scene of the crime, you know,' he said as if to an equal, 'just in case we missed something.'

The boys scuffed around in the grass. 'Don't think so,' they said 'We've looked everywhere.'

'Not found anything?'

They shook their heads. He grimaced and strolled on towards the spot where the body had been discovered. The boys skipped alongside him digging in the grass and gorse, ever hopeful of turning up a vital clue.

The grown-up reached the point he was aiming for and stood there for a moment watching them. They had turned over every clump and tussock. Sharp-eyed, methodical boys they were, reared on a diet of police stories. They probably knew how to investigate a case better than he did. If there was anything there to find they would turn it up.

\* \* \*

He looked around. Apart from the two boys the hillside was deserted. The great sweep of the ridge was marked with bare earth, the spine of the hill being swept clean by the eroding winds. The narrow grey footpath meandered in a wide zig-zag to the top, then disappeared into a cerulean void. Below him lay the spread of the dale, crowded with small dwellings each climbing on the back of the one below it. The scars of the mines were etched deep into the valley floor, the dark pit-wheels standing out like iron watch-towers shadowing the little community that huddled at their feet.

Suddenly his attention was attracted by one of the boys tugging at his sleeve. He looked down at a small freckled face bright with excitement.

'I found this.'

The hand held out contained a folding match-card, the sort distributed in restaurants and hotels. Gingerly the sergeant took it from him and turned it over.

It had now spent some time half-buried in the earth and the lettering was worn but it was possible to read the address — a restaurant in Salisbury.

'He might have thrown it away,' suggested the one boy.

'It could have fallen from his pocket,' chimed in the other.

Sergeant Knutter opened the folder. All the matches had been spent and broken off.

'It could indeed,' he declared sportingly. 'It's a clue anyway.'

'Is it an important clue?' cried the boy who had found it, dancing up and down with excitement.

Sergeant Knutter grinned with satisfaction and pocketed the evidence. 'I'll say it is,' he told them cheerfully, 'It's the only clue we've got.'

The boys fell back in amazed admiration at their own skill in detection and immediately dashed off to spread the news. The policeman watched them go with an indulgent smile. They had played their part in a great adventure and were heroes in their own eyes. That was a good start in life for anyone. Sharp-witted boys, they spent a lot of time out on the hillside expending their restless energy. It would be useful to keep in touch with them. He turned again and surveyed the landscape. The truth is always there for those that have eyes to see it.

Assuming that the man had left the path at the top of the hill where it turned back on itself and changed direction he had chosen to cross the heath presumably as a short cut to his destination. Sergeant Knutter followed the track of his supposed route with his eyes to the spot where he stood and turning carried it on in a straight line. His gaze came up against a garden wall and the shattered windows of the blasted house — the McNamara's cottage.

He felt the match-card in his pocket and turned away thoughtfully to retrace his path to town. A pattern was beginning to emerge.

# 7

Mark turned the card over in his hand and tried to decipher the address. It was beginning to snow, big, soft flakes falling on his eyelashes making it difficult to see. He brushed them away and examined the card again with the help of a street lamp. '*Colebrook*', it looked like. '*Brodribb Park Avenue.*'

He looked round and was startled to come face to face with an old woman peering at him through the lace curtains of her living room which looked directly on to the street. He held up the card and pointed at it, then shrugged his shoulders to indicate he was lost. She peered at the card, then shook her head and motioned him to come to the door.

The small terraced houses had front doors that opened into the living room so it was seconds before she stood on the front step. Mark towered over her. 'I'm lost,' he said helplessly.

She took her reading glasses out of her pocket, perched them on her nose and scanned the card briefly.

'Mr. Kelsey's place,' she said forthrightly, recognising the address, 'What would you be wanting him for?'

Mark felt he could hardly tell her to mind her own business. She must have been eighty and he needed her help.

'I'm a journalist,' he explained 'I'm hoping he can help me with an article I have to write.'

The old woman looked at him sharply. 'What sort of article?'

Mark gestured vaguely. 'Economics.'

'Not scandal?'

He smiled. 'Hardly. Financial page.'

She sniffed a little. She was still judging him. 'Help you how?'

Mark shifted a little uncomfortably. He was not used to being interrogated. So that's how the boot felt on the other foot.

'Tell me about the important people in the town. Who's who.'

'Oh, that,' she said, returning the card to him, 'I can tell you that.'

Mark tossed her what was left of his

charm, given that the cold had depressed most of it. 'I'm sure you can, Mrs . . . ?'

'Breedon. Lily Breedon.'

'Mrs. Breedon. I'd be glad to come and talk to you some time, if I may. Just right now I've got an appointment with Mr. Kelsey. I don't want to be late. It seems rude not to be on time.'

She nodded approvingly as he guessed she would. 'Keep right on, cross the railway bridge, then first right by the park. Can't miss it. Swanky sort of house for a socialist, if you ask me.'

Mark laughed at her expression. 'You don't like him?'

She jerked her head impatiently. 'It's not only the employers that live off the backs of the men, to my way of thinking.'

Mark looked reproachful. 'Not Mr. Kelsey surely?'

'Too many friends with foreign sounding names my husband used to say and he was a union man all his life. Wait till you see his house and then look at mine and think on. You know what I mean, Mr . . . ?'

Mark grinned. 'McNamara. Irish, I'm afraid.'

'North or South?'

'North. London that is.'

'It was your house that blew up.'

'My wife's . . . my ex-wife's . . . ' he paused wondering if that was quite the way to describe the woman whose bed he was sharing in the one hotel in Ravenhill.

'I just wondered when you said you were Irish.'

'Not that Irish. My great-grandfather came from Kilkenny. Gas main they think,' he lied cheerfully.

She shook her head sorrowfully and clucked her tongue. 'Never do a job properly these days.'

'That's a fact,' he agreed. 'Thanks for your help. I'll come and see you again, if I may.'

'You want to know anything,' she said with a hint of suggestiveness, as she closed the door, 'you come and ask me.'

Mark turned up his collar and stamped off in the direction she had advised him satisfied that he had made a useful contact. Her parting shot was probably no idle boast. Ravenhill was a small town, the sort of community that thrived on local gossip and Mrs. Breedon with her discreet lace curtains and sharp, penetrating eyes would undoubtedly have her finger on the pulse of things. Besides it would give a good angle. The pensioner's view.

The park, named after one late Councillor Brodribb, was more of a long garden bordering the river bank. The line of fine chestnuts that had been planted along the river walk were covered in snow as if, like the furniture in an unused house, they had had sheets thrown over them. The narrow playing field was blanketed already, the little wrought-iron bandstand shimmered like an ice mosque, its Eastern dome silhouetted against the freezing indigo sky.

Brodribb Park Avenue ran, as the name suggests alongside the linear park. It was a broad street, well planted with trees and shrubs. The houses, on one side only to ensure a view of the park and river, stood well back in splendid gardens. For the most part they were mock-tudor mansions of the Thirties interspersed by the odd spanish villa and modern bungalow. 'Colebrook' turned out to be one of the latter, a long, low building in pale grey stone, almost hidden by a bank of rhododendrons. Evidently Mr. Kelsey did not care for the view of the park, or else did not care to come under public scrutiny.

Mark was admitted to the house by an elderly housekeeper who ushered him into the living room, then discreetly disappeared. The living room was large and comfortably furnished with one wall taken up by a patio window looking out on to the garden. It was here that his host stood with his back to him watching the falling snow. As Mark entered he sensed his presence behind him and turned round.

The two men stared at each other. Edward Kelsey was the man Mark had thrown out of his house, his wife's 'friend.'

He was shorter than his guest and well into his sixties. His grey hair was still thick and swept back sleekly off his face.

He was not and probably never had been a handsome man. His features were too bold, his skin heavily lined. His face reminded Mark of a rocky landscape, the ridge of his long nose being the most prominent outcrop. His mouth, quite small in comparison, was overlapped by a neat, grey moustache. Physically he had a shrunken look about him, common to most men of his age who are not fat, but he had magnificent eyes.

It was the eyes that held Mark's attention now. They were arresting. The darkest brown, almost black, they gleamed with a warmth that drew the watcher to him like a magnet. Suddenly Mark saw what must have attracted Lou to him and also how he had dominated men for going on half a century. This ugly little man had a dangerous charm.

Seeing Mark's astonished expression he smiled. 'I'm sorry if I have startled you Mr. McNamara,' he said in soft tones, 'but I was afraid that if I told you where we had already met you wouldn't have come and I wanted to speak to you.'

'About my wife?' Mark was on his

guard. He didn't quite know why. Kelsey nodded. 'The other day. I could see how you read the situation but I want you to know you are wrong. My . . . concern for your wife was merely friendship. One lame duck to another.'

'Are you a lame duck?' Mark was aware that he was being aggressive but he found he couldn't help himself.

'We all have our deserts to cross,' replied Kelsey smoothly.

'And Lou?'

'She is lonely. I am lonely. We have something in common. So we are friends. Nothing more.'

'So she said.'

'And you believe her?'

Mark ignored the question. He was not prepared to discuss his emotions with this man. Sensing his reluctance Edward Kelsey turned politely away and went to pour him a drink.

'She was very upset,' he went on, over his shoulder, 'I was trying to console her. Scotch all right?'

'Thank you. What was she upset about?'

'You, I imagine. It was a considerable shock to her when you turned up out of the blue.'

Mark accepted the proffered glass ruefully. 'I suppose it was,' he admitted.

'What I can't understand,' said Mr. Kelsey bluntly, 'is why you left her in the first place. She's a marvellous woman. She has the kind of eyes that stir a man's soul — like the sea, unknown depths that a man could drown in, hidden currents, flashes of light, creation, music, poetry, all the happiness we ever dream of, all in a woman's eyes.'

'You sound as if you're in love with her,' objected Mark pettishly.

Kelsey laughed. 'I'm not saying I'm not. I'm not too old to dream, you know. All I'm saying is your suspicions are groundless. I just can't understand why you walked out on her, that's all.'

Mark scowled. 'What is this? Marriage Guidance Council?'

Edward Kelsey scratched his head. 'Just call it curiosity.'

'It wasn't all my fault,' Mark burst out suddenly, annoyed by the older man's air of self-righteousness. 'She wouldn't give up her job. I needed to change mine. It took up all her time. It takes two you know . . . '

He faltered, wishing he hadn't said so much. He felt he was being manouvered into betraying himself in some way.

Mr. Kelsey didn't press him. 'She had a very good job, I gather. Computers, wasn't it?'

Mark nodded. 'A dehumanising profession, if you ask me.'

'Dangerous things computers,' murmered Mr. Kelsey 'Very impersonal. Anyway she's given that all up now.'

Mark looked puzzled. 'I suppose she must have done. I never thought to ask. That surprises me. She was so dead set on a career.'

'Perhaps,' intoned Mr. Kelsey philosophically, 'she has come to realise there is more to life than ambition.'

Mark laughed suddenly. 'Do you believe that?'

Mr. Kelsey smiled indulgently. 'I've retired, haven't I?'

'Have you?' There was a slight change

in Mark's tone, the reporter re-surfacing.

'I have.'

'I thought old socialists were like old actors. They went on till they dropped. What made you give up?'

Kelsey pursed his lips and looked at the ceiling before giving his answer. 'The face of socialism is changing in this country. I am, as you say, an old socialist. I know what you're going to say . . . ' he waved Mark to silence as he opened his mouth, 'I was as left-wing in my time as any. Not so. I was not a Communist you know, *never* a communist. I have always believed in a democratic labour movement. Government of the people by the people and all that. I'm a bit of a romantic, I dare say.'

'I've never heard you called that!'

'There's a new breed of socialist — that *call* themselves socialist, that I don't like the look of. I don't like their faces because they don't care to show them. I don't like their words because they say one thing when they mean another. They talk softly of destruction. I don't like that.'

'They say the same things, don't they?' remarked Mark cynically 'Trot out the same old arguments?'

Kelsey shook his head. 'In my day socialists were poor men who hated poverty. Now they are wealthy men who hate wealth. Why is that? I ask myself'

'You tell me.' Mark shifted a little uncomfortably. He wondered if this was going to be a long speech. He had not come for a political discussion.

'Because wealth is power and ambitious men can't stand to see power in other hands. They want it all for themselves.' Kelsey sighed. 'There's no place for men like me anymore — foolish romantics with the Robin Hood mentality. Socialism used to be the politics of social justice, now its the politics of envy. So I've retired.'

'Is that wise? With the revolution pending?'

'The revolution will be the death of the Labour movement. It will be the death of old ideals, of common humanity and social responsibility. It will be the end of the little man's chance to better himself.

I'm a preacher, you know, a man of Christian views. Politics and morality go hand in hand in my book.'

'You *are* a romantic,' Mark observed drily.

'Yes. Another drink?'

Mark nodded. The whisky had begun to course through him sweeping aside the chill of the night. He handed his glass over for a refill.

'They don't like it, of course,' went on Edward Kelsey as he poured out the spirit. 'The Labour movement is rooted deeply in its traditions. In many ways it is *the* conservative party. The tradition of parliamentary liberties for example. It's a matter of genetics as much as principle. Freedom is in the blood. When the older generation like myself start turning our backs on the new Left they start feeling the cold, but I for one will not pass on the mantle to cover their shame.'

'They think you should support them out of loyalty to the cause.'

'Cause,' sneered the older man, 'Causes go hand in hand with effects. You have to study the one to judge the other. I'll not join the other side. I've been a leopard too long to change my spots now, but I'll not endorse facism.'

'You think it's as bad as that?'

'Socialism is just a name. It's what you do that makes you what you are. Hitler called himself a socialist, never forget that.'

Mark took the glass he handed to him and sipped the drink thoughtfully. Edward Kelsey was going to a lot of trouble to establish his innocence. Was it just for something to say or a desire not to be misunderstood or had he some other reason?

'Something's just occured to me,' Mark said slowly, 'you were there.'

'There?' Kelsey looked up sharply. 'Where?'

'When the house blew up,' said Mark sourly.

'Blew up?'

'Didn't you hear? Lou's house blew up.'

'My God!'

'Fortunately we weren't in it at the time or there would have been a nasty mess, but just before the jolly old balloon went up you were there, too.'

Edward Kelsey looked at him warily. 'What are you suggesting?'

Mark looked up, blandly innocent. 'That makes three, doesn't it?'

'Three?'

'Possible victims. Lou, me and you.'

'My God!' Edward Kelsey sat down heavily and gulped his Scotch.

'Makes you think, doesn't it?' observed Mark genially.

★   ★   ★

Sergeant Knutter put down the telephone receiver. That was that. He had traced every single blessed restaurant, hotel and café in Salisbury and not one bore the name on the match card. He had no idea how long it had been lying on the heath. Possibly it was an old piece of litter and the company who issued it had long gone out of business but he had had a hunch about it. He sniffed forlornly. So much for intuition. It was not likely to produce any fresh leads after all.

He tossed the telephone book into the desk-drawer and reached for his coat. Another blank drawn it was time to have a drink and see what philosophy could do.

# 8

The hotel room was pale and without character. Even with the curtains open the narrow sash window admitted only a faint drift of wintry sunlight that seemed to have had all the heat drawn out of it. The cream walls changed colour only fractionally where the light touched them. Cream bedspreads matched their blandness. There was no picture in the room, only a blank television screen. The decor was designed to project anonymity.

Lou picked up Mark's clothes from the floor where he had left them and lovingly folded them, placing them in a neat pile on the end of the bed. It was strange how the old habits came back to her as if they had never been away.

She still loved him. She could not forget how her heart had jumped at the sight of him. It was a moment of sheer joy even after all those months, even after he had deserted her . . . Deserted — that was a cruel word conjuring up the barren waste her life had been reduced to, the hopelessness of an empty horizon. No future, nothing to look forward to, just the day by day trudge through a searing landscape of bitter loneliness.

She had faced up to all that, resigned herself even. She had struggled to get her little home together, built out of the ruins of the old one and now, just as she was beginning to feel a surer foundation under her feet the whole thing had been blown apart, her little house wrecked, her plans for the future sent spinning in to the void and the horizon was again blurred and uncertain.

Lou sat down and wept. There was nothing in this cold, expressionless little room to comfort her. Instinctively she picked up Mark's clothes and hugged them to her, seeming to draw some warmth from them. Then she let them fall again. He had not come back for her — he had admitted as much. It was an accident. Foolish to make any plans. What was she to do then? She was running scared. He still had a power over her that frightened her. When she saw him again she should have felt anger, bitterness, cold hatred even when all she had felt was an absurd, unquenchable happiness. She loved him. She needed him. She was prepared to forgive everything if he would come back and start again. The question was could she trust him?

★ ★ ★

The little town had settled under a thick blanket of snow. Grey and white in neat little squares and grid patterns blocked by the great whorling swirl of the hillsides — an impressionist painter's dream. The river ran chattering through the valley, not hardened yet, although it carried great chunks of impacted snow and frozen branches glittering with icicles. There were few people in the streets and they were well muffled like Breugel peasants, tramping along in wellingtons or thick sheepskin boots.

Mark had neither in his suitcase so he slithered precariously on thin soles and felt his feet gradually absorbing the cold wet until they were so cold he could scarcely feel anything at all. It had not been a rewarding morning. He had interviewed several members of the Chamber of Commerce who all said the same thing. Business was bad and the future as bleak as the weather. The employers blamed the workers, the workers blamed the management and everybody blamed the government. Mark sighed. There was nothing new there to appeal to his editor. It would make a change if some of them blamed themselves.

The door of the pub stood ajar. He hesitated. Lou would be waiting for him. A pleasing odour of beer, meat pies and cigarette smoke wafted from the dark shadows within the door. His feet were soaking. Making a sudden decision he pushed open the door and went in. A sudden wall of heat hit his body like a physical blow. The pleasure was acutely sensual. A massive log-fire burned in the eternal half-light of the bar which was packed with bodies generating the warm cosiness of companionship irresistible to a man coming in from the cold. The glasses gleamed invitingly. The barmaid smiled a welcome.

He bought a pint, then went to warm his feet by the fire, bagging one of the Windsor chairs as soon as someone vacated it. He sat there for a few moments toasting his toes. It was heavenly bliss.

'Any luck, Sir?' a voice interrupted his reverie.

He looked up to see Sergeant Knutter towering above him, leaning on the huge mantelpiece of the old inglenook fireplace.

'Any luck?'

'With your investigations. Into the state of the economy.'

'No. None at all. No one has anything new to say.'

Sergeant Knutter moved to deposit his bulk in a newly vacated seat and pulled it round opposite the journalist to converse more comfortably with him.

'How about you?' asked Mark lazily, still half-concentrating on the delicious tingle the fire had wrought in his frozen toes.

The policeman shook his head. 'Complete blank. Whichever way you look.'

'Nothing to go on?'

They were joined by Chris Williams, carrying the beer for his colleague and himself. No seat being available he was obliged to stand.

Sergeant Knutter felt in his pocket and produced the tattered match-card. 'Only this,' he said, handing it over for Mark to examine, 'but I've tracked down every single restaurant and café in Salisbury and there's not one of that name.'

'I know this,' said Mark suddenly sitting up. 'I know where it is.'

'Know it?'

'The Grey Goose. Salisbury. Yes. I'm sure I know where it is.'

'Well!' Sergeant Knutter sat back in astonishment. 'That's more than the Wiltshire police could tell me. They've never heard of it.'

'Wiltshire?' Mark looked blankly up at him for a moment. 'Not Wiltshire. Zimbabwe.'

'Zimbabwe?'

Sergeant Knutter and Inspector Williams exchanged glances. Chris Williams whistled softly. 'The African connection?' he queried.

'The what?' Mark creased his forehead in a puzzled frown.

'Nothing,' said Inspector Williams hastily, 'but how did you come to know of this place?'

'I've been there,' replied Mark simply.

'Recently?'

'Some time ago. A year or so. My wife's . . . ' he hesitated suddenly, then went on slowly, staring at the match-card as if seeing it properly for the first time. 'My wife's company invited us out there. Their headquarters is in Salisbury.'

'What sort of company would that be?'

Mark grimaced. 'Import-export, I suppose you'd call it. They deal mainly in computer software. Business systems. Programs for payrolls, invoicing, accounts, personnel records, that sort of thing. It's the coming thing. At least, that's what I gather. I've never taken much interest, I'm afraid.'

Sergeant Knutter took the crumpled

card from his fingers and restored it to his pocket.

'Thank you very much, Sir. That gives us something to think about. Salisbury, Zimbabwe. I'd never have thought of that. It's a good thing to mix with a man who's well-travelled.'

'Where does it get us though?' mused Inspector Williams aloud.

'Would you like me to go out there?' Sergeant Knutter offered helpfully, 'Show his picture around. Someone might identify him.'

Chris Williams gave a crack of laughter.

'You've been watching too much television. We'll send it to the Salisbury police if you like, see if they can match it to one of their mug-shots and we can try the embassy, see if any of their nationals have gone missing in this country. That's the best we can do on our budget.'

'Pity,' murmured Sergeant Knutter, contentedly supping his beer, 'I've always had a fancy to see Africa.'

The bomb blast had forced a huge jagged hole in the front living-room wall so that the interior of the house was now exposed to the street. The window frame had been pushed out of position and balanced precariously on the broad sill. There was no glass left in it. The door hung itself half off its hinges, its panels cracked and splintered. The milk bottles waiting for collection had been miraculously untouched.

Lou stepped gingerly over the rubble. The snow had drifted through the hole and soaked what was left of the carpet. It had settled on the furniture. It seemed strange — almost surreal — to be standing inside the house looking through the wall at the snowy street and to see snow on the furniture . . .

Lou ran her fingers through her hair in a despairing gesture. The mess was awful. Pictures had fallen from the walls. The drawers of the dresser had been blown open and papers were fluttering across the room. A cushion she had carefully embroidered was a mass of filthy shreds. That brought tears to her eyes for some reason. Her wedding photograph . . .

She picked up the twisted frame and tried to withdraw the charred picture. She and Mark stood side by side in the formal pose of happiness but their faces were unrecognisable, her lovely white dress stained brown. Sadly she let the photograph flutter from her fingers and join the rest of the litter.

She didn't know where to start. The room looked as if a team of careless burglars had turned it over and ripped it apart. She moved around shifting odd sticks of furniture — sticks being the operative word — and re-arranging the piles of rubble into smaller neater piles of rubble. After twenty-five minutes she still hadn't got anywhere.

'Can I come in?'

She turned around abruptly. Sergeant Knutter stood in the gaping doorway peering beneath the sagging lintel. She gestured helplessly.

'There's nothing to stop you, is there?'

He stepped over the threshold. 'Bit of a shambles.'

Lou nodded and brushed away the

tears. The presence of another person gave her the motivation to face her disaster stoically.

'I don't know where to start,' she confessed, forcing a tight laugh.

He smiled sympathetically. 'Suppose we board the gap up a bit? Stop the weather coming in?'

She nodded gratefully. He had a big man's ability to exude strength in a crisis.

'There's some hardboard out the back, I think.'

'Good,' he said in a cheerful, practical tone 'See if you can find a hammer, will you?'

He went through the house picking his way delicately, almost fastidiously through the wreckage. She sorted through the dresser drawers. She knew there was a hammer there somewhere.

When he came back with the hardboard she had found it and handed it to him with a tin of nails.

He quickly hammered the hardboard in position across the yawning hole. It didn't quite fit but it had the effect of shutting the street from view. Only small gaps of daylight were visible. Lou found an old curtain which she tacked up to cover these. He pulled the shattered door to and while this enclosed them in semi-darkness it seemed to help to restore a sense of privacy to the room.

'You're insured, I suppose?' he asked, by way of conversation.

Lou spread her arms helplessly. 'I'm not sure. Fire and so on, yes. Even Acts of God, all the usual things, but bomb damage? One never reads the small print.'

'A bit unexpected this lot.' It was a statement rather than a question but she didn't answer in any case.

'It's all the little things,' she burst out suddenly, anger mingled with pain and disbelief, 'all the silly things that can't be replaced. The photographs, ornaments, silly little bits and pieces that mark the landscape of your life, all blown to pieces . . . ' The tears began to flow. She could hold them back no longer. 'They all mean so much don't they?'

'They do,' he said evenly. 'Some things are beyond value. Corny but true.'

The tears were rolling down her

cheeks. Her dark blue eyes were wet with them. He paused to consider what a beautiful woman she was. She met his gaze. He was regarding her with dispassionate interest. Heartlessness or merely professional curiosity?

'I came for some clothes really,' she said abruptly, forcing herself to be matter-of-fact.

'Mind those stairs,' he said sharply as she turned towards them 'are they safe?'

The stairs were built in the centre of the house. To climb them one had to step through what appeared to be a cupboard. The door had lost all its centre panels. It looked absurd, an empty frame. Lou didn't bother to open it. She stepped through the hole and peered cautiously upwards.

'I think so,' she said after a brief inspection. 'I'm not heavy.'

'You go carefully,' he admonished her severely. 'The beams may be weakened. We don't want you falling through the ceiling.'

She started to laugh and cry at the same time. As if the ceiling mattered.

Upstairs the bedroom was undamaged. The vibration of the explosion had scattered her belongings from the dressing-table but compared to the debris downstairs the room was fairly tidy. A chair had fallen over. She straightened this and picked up one or two of the bottles and jars that had rolled across the carpet. She noticed the mirror of the dressing-table was cracked from end to end but it had not shattered.

'Seven years bad luck,' she thought to herself then laughed at the absurdity of her superstition. There was no glass at all in the window.

She pulled the curtains across to shut out the cold wind and seizing a holdall began to stuff clothes into it. As an afterthought she picked up one or two things Mark had left lying around and pushed them into a carrier bag. Mercifully he had left most of his luggage in the car at the time the bomb went off so he still had it with him.

She scrambled back down the stairs where Sergeant Knutter was patiently waiting for her, anxiously watching for any sign of strain in the building.

'Got everything?' he asked a trifle impatiently as if it were only a matter of collecting a toothbrush.

She nodded then cast her eyes over the dismantled room again. She knelt and retrieved her embroidered cushion, black and ragged though it now was, and thoughtfully placed it in the one remaining armchair, plumping it into shape as if, like a good housewife, she could not bear to go out of the house and leave it untidy.

'Why did it happen to me?' mused Sergeant Knutter aloud, speaking her thoughts for her.

She made no reply.

'Of course you know why, don't you?'

She spun round. A subtle, professional tone had crept into his voice. The fringe of her hair fell across her eyes which burned accusingly beneath it. His placid gaze didn't waver. The pale blue of his eyes seemed to glaze over his thoughts so she couldn't read what he was thinking although the points of fire blazed as ever.

'What do you mean by that?' she demanded belligerently.

He smiled in his gentle, genial way.

'That man found on the heath.'

'What about him?'

'You know who he was, Mrs. McNamara. Don't you?'

# 9

The two boys crouched at the very far end of the platform where it began to slope down on to the line. Ahead of them the tracks fanned out, some disappearing into sidings protected by cavernous sheds, some coming to a dead end marked by rusty buffers and those central tracks that ran into the long platform following the bend that would take them along the main line south to London. The boys crouched, poised to leap up every time a fast blue train flashed through the station ready to sight the engine number and scribble it furiously into the little note-books they carried.

The station in the snow was a fine geometric pattern of black and white. Here and there workmen in yellow protective coats stepped among the sleepers and an enormous hoarding incongruously pictured an island paradise populated apparently by bikinied girls.

Apart from these it was a colourless scene. The platform was deserted except for the two boys, who had begun to get restless. It was cold and the train was a long time coming.

'Last one?' suggested the red-haired lad.

'Only got half a page,' protested his companion.

'I promised me mam,' urged the first boy 'She'll give us hell if we're late.'

The dark-haired boy nodded agreement. He well understood the pressures of domestic life.

'Wait for this'n though. Thisn'ts London express.'

They waited. The whole station, it seemed, waited, caught between breaths. There was a stillness about it, almost a hush of anticipation. Then came a whine down the line and a shuddering vibration gathered momentum.

'She's coming,' whooped the dark boy.

The ginger lad didn't answer but stood shading his eyes, looking down the track. After a moment or two he pointed as the yellow face of the train showed itself round the bend.

It came with a rush, then a squeal of brakes as it slowed into the platform and stopped, panting. The station came alive with a banging of doors, the babble of voices and the clatter of feet as the carriages disgorged their passengers, who flooded as a body towards the ticket barrier. The two boys jotted the number into their books and made off after them to the comparative warmth of the entrance hall. Here they were confronted by two gentlemen.

The boys eyed them curiously as they might greet aliens from another planet for these men were Londoners, city dwellers from the mysterious teeming south.

The first of them was a tall, thin man, immaculately attired in a dark pin stripe suit. He carried a black briefcase, the sort without handles, designed for documents, a long, furled umbrella and . . . yes, he carried a bowler hat although he did not wear it.

His face was smooth like a woman's, and an unusual shape, a long, elliptical face like an egg. His hair was also smooth, sleekly tailored to the outline of the egg. Only his ears stuck out like jug handles. His eyebrows, like his hair, were silver grey and finely arched so that he bore a permanently startled expression. His nose was long and narrow, smooth like a blade, and his eyes were a pale, opaque green like a couple of coggies. He looked the perfect silly ass.

His height ensured that he caught the eye but he moved also with a consciously graceful step. He did not walk. He glided along drawing all eyes to him. He was altogether a smooth character.

His companion was less interesting. He was a small, well-dressed businessman in a blue lounge suit. He carried the usual executive attaché case and a small plastic bag in which he kept his sandwiches and litter. He walked with a hurried step, partly out of habit and partly in order to keep up with his long-legged escort. He appeared to be the kind of man who is always between meetings.

The boys eyed these two strange specimens curiously. The tall one beckoned them and spoke to them in the drawling, dandified accents that they had hitherto associated only with actors on television. They exchanged glances and tried to smother a laugh.

'Po-lice station,' repeated the man loudly and clearly, carefully enunciating each syllable as if he were talking to idiots or foreigners.

'Police station, mister?' asked one of the boys cheekily 'What would you be wanting there?'

The tall man regarded him with the sweet expression of the utterly exasperated. 'I am a double agent working with the MI5. My friend here is an arms dealer on his way to Northern Ireland. We wish to give ourselves up.'

The boys gave him the look that children reserve for idiot grown-ups.

'You want to know the way?'

'Yes,' said the tall man simply, 'Where is it?'

'I canna tell thee just like that,' protested the ginger lad, slipping into the soft, quick slurred speech of the district, partly in self-defence and partly out of bloody-mindedness.

'Then show me,' suggested the tall man

patiently, 'if it won't take you too far out of your way.'

'Oh, no,' admitted the boy cheerfully, 'It's on us way. We can show thee right enough.'

'Good,' said the man closing the deal, 'I suppose fifty pence each will adequately recompense you for your trouble?'

He handed each boy a coin which they received eagerly. He smiled a sly, superior smile as if he had known all along the natives could be bought with baubles. Not such a silly ass after all. He gestured them to lead on. Whither they went the two men followed.

\* \* \*

Mark stood in the back-yard holding a smooth plank of timber and watched Lou as she made her way up the hillside. He had come to help her clear up the mess and make a more secure job of boarding up the damaged wall than the temporary barrier improvised by Sergeant Knutter. She had found the business of counting the cost of the shattered furniture and broken ornaments too upsetting and had gone for a walk by herself for a bit. He let her go. It would do her more good than moping around.

The sky was a clear transluscent blue. The snow clouds had, for the moment, drifted on, leaving the hills like upturned pudding-bowls, a series of smooth, white hemispheres. A brilliant sun shone like a hard new penny. Everything was clean-cut and marked by the brightness it reflected. It would make a good advertisement for washing-powder, he decided idly, or toothpaste. Fresh white and tingling snow always for some reason or other put him in mind of laundry — of sheets draped over the knees of some mountainous giant, of bodies wrapped together hidden from prying eyes. He smiled at his own fancy. When the snow came it would be like a pillow-fight again, feathers flying everywhere.

He watched as Lou climbed the steep side of the hill, leaving a trail of dark footsteps in the virgin snow meandering behind her. He could pick her out easily. She was wearing blue jeans and a dark blue duffle coat. A long green scarf trailed over her shoulder. He could pick her out anyway by her lovely red hair, very striking against the white snow.

He kept his eyes on her until he saw she had reached the path safely, then he picked up his plank and went back into the jumbled house where his boarded wall was half-complete. He would finish what he was doing and then he would follow her.

★   ★   ★

The two men took their seats in Inspector Williams' office. It was a small room, mainly occupied by a plain light-wood desk. The walls were a dull sage green and a green blind filtered the weak sunlight. There was barely enough room for four bodies.

The taller of the two visitors placed his briefcase on his knees in the manner of a woman cradling her shopping basket and held out his hand.

'Sellingby,' he said by way of self-introduction, 'Marcus Sellingby.' Inspector

Williams had to twist himself across the desk to shake his hand.

'And this,' said Mr. Sellingby, indicating his companion, 'is Mr. Harrap.' Inspector Williams performed his contortion again then sat down facing them. Sergeant Knutter stood by the door as if he were guarding it.

'The powers that be,' went on Mr. Sellingby, his marbled eyes betraying nothing at all, 'have sent us to help you with your little problem.'

Inspector Williams cast a speculative glance over them. 'Special Branch?' Mr. Sellingby smiled indulgently. 'Nothing so glamorous, I'm afraid. MOD. Department WS stroke eleven J, if that means anything to you.'

Inspector Williams shook his head. Sellingby didn't bother to enlighten him.

'This . . . ' he continued helpfully, pointing again to his silent fellowtraveller, 'is Mr. Harrap of EDS Limited.'

'EDS?' queried the inspector.

'Electronic Defence Systems,' supplied Mr. Harrap in a tight, reluctant voice.

'Burglar alarms, sir?' inquired Sergeant

Knutter with professional interest.

Marcus Sellingby gave a crack of laughter and slapped his thigh. 'Burglar alarms, Harrap! That's very good. I like that.'

Mr. Harrap permitted himself a restricted smile. 'Not exactly,' he said patiently. 'Weapons Inspector. We make guided weapons — the homing and guidance elements at any rate. The casings, of course, are made by National Aerospace Incorporated.'

'Under licence from the MOD of course,' purred Mr. Sellingby full of selfsatisfaction.

'What does this have to do with our investigations?' asked Inspector Williams bluntly, cradling a biro between his fingers with a view to jotting information down but so far not employing it.

'Your late gentleman found on the hillside.'

'Yes?'

'Well, you tell me . . . ' Sellingby smiled invitingly.

Williams shrugged. 'Can't be much help to you, I'm afraid. We don't even know who he is.'

'Oh, we know who he is,' exclaimed Sellingby smugly. 'We know who he is all right.'

'Would you mind telling us?' Inspector Williams was beginning to feel mildly irritated by these smooth city gents with their secretive smiles and evident satisfaction in playing their war-games.

As if he divined his opinion Marcus Sellingby became suddenly brisk and business like.

'Geoff Randall. Geoffrey Stephen Randall. You like full names, don't you?' He unzipped his document case and fished out a plain manilla file. 'All the details are there.' he handed it to the policeman. 'It saves going through it all verbally, don't you think? However, the case is not quite closed, although we know who he was and what he was involved in.'

'What?' asked Williams shortly. He felt humbled having to ask for information when he had none to offer himself. It looked like inefficiency.

Mr. Sellingby pressed his fingers together and pursed his lips as if deciding how to begin. He went to the door and checked outside then resumed his seat again.

'This . . . what we are going to say now . . . must not go outside this room, Inspector.'

Williams nodded.

'Sergeant?'

'As a drum, sir.'

'Good. Official Secrets Act and all that, you understand. Have you heard, either of you, of Xanadu?'

'In Xanadu did Kubla Khan a stately pleasure-dome decree,' intoned Sergeant Knutter, adding as an afterthought, 'sir.'

'Well done, Sergeant,' declared Sellingby, adding some measured applause. 'If you will remember it goes on later:

'A mighty fountain momently was forced
    amid whose swift half-intermitted burst
    Huge fragments vaulted like rebounding hail': Inspired images. Harrap'd better explain.'

The two policemen looked politely to the nervous businessman. He coughed once or twice then took the floor.

'EDS Limited recently completed the concept and international programme definition phase of a Terminal Guidance Warhead for a Multiple Rocket Launch System which we have code-named Xanadu.'

'Come again?'

'The Xanadu system,' said Harrap carefully, leaning forward as if he were imparting a tit-bit of 'confidential' gossip, 'is a defensive network of ground-to-air missiles that, when in position, will provide London, or any major city come to that, with complete protective cover from air or ground-based missile attack. The effect will be the same as if the city were covered by a vast impenetrable dome.'

'It was a miracle of rare device.

A sunny pleasure-dome with caves of ice,' chanted Sellingby. 'Xanadu you see?'

'And 'mid this tumult Kubla heard from far Ancestral voices prophesying war,' added Sergeant Knutter thoughtfully.

'Exactly,' agreed Sellingby prosaically. 'Can't be too careful, can you?'

'EDS Limited have developed the system and will be the principal manufacturers,' pointed out Harrap with some pride.

'Under licence,' put in Sellingby.

'From the MOD,' Williams finished the sentence for him, 'but what has this Xanadu system got to do with our late anonymous friend, or shouldn't I ask?'

Sellingby smiled. 'The Xanadu system,' he said like a salesman, 'is the most advanced, the most highly developed defensive system in the world. Its missiles will have ten times the capability of any other ground-to-air missiles at present on the market.' He might have been talking of soap powder. 'It is brilliantly conceived, flawless in its design and above all it is British.'

'Rule Britannia,' commented the policeman drily.

Sellingby's smile flickered indulgently at his simplicity. 'Aside from the military advantage such a system would give us, the commercial prospects are devastating. The final contracts have not been negotiated yet, of course, but this government alone is contemplating an investment in the region of seven hundred million. NATO is certain to be involved in the project giving prospective sales of . . . oh, say a minimum of six thousand million.'

Inspector Williams looked impressed. 'That's a lot of bread.'

'Unfortunately, like all highly technological developments the very intricate nature of its construction means that it is prone to be . . . well . . . vulnerable in key areas.'

'What does that mean?'

'It can go wrong,' translated Knutter.

'No,' Sellingby held up a hand to contradict him, 'it cannot go wrong — that is the beauty of the system. Whereas a human guard may sleep, or commit an error of judgement, the Xanadu is a round-the-clock watchman who never makes a mistake. It's infallible.'

'Then what's the snag?'

'Guided Missile Systems,' interrupted Harrap solemnly, 'are highly dependent on software.'

Inspector Williams looked at him quizzically.

'He means they're run by computers,' explained Sellingby kindly, stifling his companions protest by adding, 'to put it in layman's terms.'

Williams nodded. 'And?'

'There are two ways of countering a guided missile attack. One is by using an anti-missile missile such as the Sea Wolf, but that is a last line of defence and extremely expensive. The other is much simpler, that is by employing jamming techniques.'

'Like radio jamming?'

'Exactly like radio jamming, in fact. One jams the frequencies that guide the homing head, confusing the co-ordinates and, one hopes causing it to land harmlessly in the sea. This is, however, a bit of a hit and miss affair unless . . . '

'Unless?'

'One knows the frequencies in advance. Then, of course, one can narrow the band and concentrate on jamming where it counts.'

'So?'

'So there we have the crux of the matter. The Xanadu system is governed by a software development which we call the Xanadu Program. The Program is responsible for the launch and homing and guidance of the Warheads. It is the key to the whole system. In other words it is no use having an umbrella in the rain if you can't get the damn thing up.' He tapped his own umbrella on the floor to emphasise his point. 'Gentlemen, I have to tell you . . . and I beg you not at this stage to tell anyone else . . . that the powers that be have lost the Xanadu Program.'

'Lost it?'

'Lost, stolen or strayed. It's the one element we simply can't afford to lose. Unless we can recover it our 'stately pleasure-dome' will be as fragile as an egg-shell.'

'You mean the defence of whole western world is at stake,' cracked Williams facetiously. 'I thought it was something important.'

'Not quite the western world,' protested Mr. Sellingby smoothly. 'We do have other weapons but a considerable amount of money and research has gone into this project. The commercial loss alone might be enough to bring down a government without the trouble of military intervention. We don't want somebody stealing our thunder anyway, do we, Harrap?'

Mr. Harrap swallowed and shook his head as though the prospect rendered him speechless.

'Geoff Randall worked for an Import-Export firm, Intercontinental Software Systems — what names these companies do have nowadays! — known as INSOFT for short. He was . . . without wishing to sound dramatic . . . one of our operatives.'

'A government agent?'

Mr. Sellingby smiled as if he found this terminology quaintly amusing. 'As you say. We believe he discovered the means whereby the Xanadu program was to be smuggled out of the country.'

'Via Salisbury, Zimbabwe,' put in Sergeant Knutter helpfully.

Mr. Sellingby's startled expression

became very pronounced.

'Salisbury . . . yes.'

'Through the company's computer links with its Head Office,' added the detective sergeant blandly.

'Precisely. How did you know?'

Sergeant Knutter smiled angelically. 'Just deduction, sir.'

Inspector Williams grinned at him. They were not such hick-detectives after all.

'Anyway,' went on Sellingby, recovering his poise, 'the man's dead now and the tapes have vanished.'

'You want our co-operation to help you find them?' Williams shuffled the papers in front of him.

'Naturally. We must recover those tapes.'

'Salisbury to Angola sir?' suggested Knutter tentatively.

'Angola or any of the other communist-backed African states. Angola to Moscow. An indirect route but I think we may safely assume that to be the destination.'

'Yes, sir.'

'Every assistance, Inspector. I trust we

can count on you?'

The young man facing him across the desk nodded obediently. Sellingby smiled appreciatively. A triumphant light flickered momentarily in his glassy eyes then disappeared like a rat down a hole. 'Sergeant?'

'Of course, sir. Every assistance, sir.'

The trouble with Knutter was you could never tell when he meant it.

# 10

Lou trudged to the top of the hill, her mind concentrated on her physical struggle. The snow was deep, almost to the top of her wellington boots in places. The smooth, inviting slopes that had seduced her to come and walk on them proved treacherous once she had foundered into their depths. She paused for breath. It was a hard climb. She looked back down at the row of little cottages behind her, their roofs sprinkled with snow like icing sugar on a cake. Here and there the shiny slate gleamed through where a heavy fall had slid down into the street. They looked a long way down. She could see her own backyard quite clearly. It was empty now. Mark had gone.

She looked up at the crest of the hill, the long spine of rock pushing up through the white body of the slope. The abrasive winds had scraped it clear of snow pushing huge drifts downwards. It was through these that Lou had to force her way. There was a long way to go up but still further to go down. There was nothing for it but to push on. It was like wading through the sea against a stiff current. Her legs began to ache.

Gaining the ridge she paused again and looked around her. The wide plateau of gently undulating moorland rolled away before her. This was what she had come to see. There was nothing to see really, just a broad expanse of white reaching as far as her field of vision, then melting into the distance into the low snow-heavy clouds that were moving slowly in her direction.

Above her the sky was still brilliantly blue. Standing above what seemed to be acres of candyfloss Lou felt the same exhilaration she did when flying. She felt as if she were standing above the clouds. A lone kestrel wheeled round her searching in vain for some signs of life and movement in the still snowscape. The sun was quite hot. Lou could feel its warmth burning her cheeks although the rest of her was cold. A spray of radiance fanned across the sky but in the distance dark fleeces began to blot out the horizon.

Lou contemplated them for a moment. Not that way, she decided. She might get lost and to be caught on the moor in a snowstorm was not anybody's idea of a good night out. Instead she turned and followed the ridge aiming to circle the town and climb back down at the other end.

From her vantage point she could see the whole ribbon-like community stretched out below her. The river traced a gleaming silver path along the valley floor, tracked by the dark still waters of the canal and a little to one side the criss-cross tracks of the railway. Classic ribbon development, she thought to herself, and remembered how she had drawn a diagram of just such a valley in her school geography book little thinking that one day she would come to live in one. Funny how rarely we relate lessons to life.

A stumpy church tower marked the beginning of the town. She would walk parallel with the High Street along the ridge, she decided, until she saw the tower directly below her, then she would come down.

She looked around her. The bright sky and the glistening snow exuded an energy, like the power given off by a rolling sea that transmits itself to everything around it. Lou began to feel the strength of it. The jumbled thoughts that had troubled her mind gave way to it. She felt her brain beginning to clear. There could be no darkness, no complications here. Here, high on the hills in the full light of the sun everything was sharp and well-defined. There was nothing to concern her but the exhilarating sense of sharing in the life, the power and the glory. Forever and ever amen, she added sentimentally. Sometimes, at moments like this, she thought there were only ever two things that really mattered — space and light.

Below her the trees in the park blossomed with ice like an apple orchard. Even in the dead grip of winter, she thought, there is something to look forward to.

She began to walk along the ridge again, hopping and skipping every now and then out of a childish urge to experiment. Every now and then she stopped and gazed all round her, trying to drink in the scene as a refreshing draught.

As she paused she noticed a silver gleam flash behind her. It came from behind a hump, where a small cairn had been erected as a war memorial. It was now just another bump in the eiderdown.

It came again. It was in an odd position for a tin can or a piece of glass. It was a sharp metallic gleam like a . . .

She began to scramble down the hillside. It was pure instinct that flung her forward into the snow. A sharp stab of fear had thrust itself into her consciousness. She fell rolling down the slope as a sharp crack was followed by a clear whine as something whistled over her.

Christ! she thought somewhat ridiculously. Someone's shooting at me.

She gave it no further thought. She half-leaped up and went rushing down the hillside. A second crack sent her flying into a small hollow where she lay panting.

121

She was not hit. She was soaked through and covered in snow but mercifully none of the dark damp patches was made by blood.

What to do now? She could stay where she was in some kind of cover although there was precious little of that. Against the white snow she was a sitting duck. She lay still for a moment hardly daring to breathe. Had the gunman seen her fall? Perhaps he thought he had succeeded and would go and leave her alone? Perhaps he was merely circling round her to get a better aim?

Instinct answered her questions for her. She was not going to wait to find out. She flung herself out of the hole and went running down the hill as fast as her legs could carry her.

\* \* \*

'Where's my wife?'

The four men looked up in surprise as McNamara burst into the police station. Two of them were just on the point of leaving.

'Where's my wife?' he repeated wildly, grabbing the inspector roughly by the arms.

'Hold on a minute,' said Williams handing him off. 'What's all this about?'

Mark ran his hand through his hair in a demented manner. 'She's gone. She's disappeared.'

★   ★   ★

'How's that, sir?' Knutter interrupted him sharply.

'She's gone,' Mark repeated loudly as if addressing a deaf man, nearly weeping with frustration. 'She went for a walk. She didn't come back, not to the cottage, nor to the hotel. I've looked everywhere.'

'Now hang on a minute,' put in Inspector Williams, taking charge of the situation. 'When did she go for a walk?'

'A few hours ago. She went up the hill behind the cottage.'

'Well then . . . '

'A few *hours* ago. She went for a short walk. She was upset what with the state of the house and everything so I let her go. I thought it would do her good to get out for a bit. She didn't come back.'

'You say she was upset,' pointed out Williams in the soothing voice that comes with frequent dealings with distressed people. 'She's probably gone to talk to a friend, or a relative maybe. She has been under a strain. She's had a terrific shock.'

Mark hesitated. The calm reassurance of the policeman seemed to reduce his anxiety to the level of a neurosis. How could he explain the sick feeling he had inside? What did that prove?

'I suppose so.' he agreed reluctantly.

'It's the most likely explanation. Nine times out of ten when people disappear they turn up later wondering what all the fuss was about. Isn't that so, Sergeant?'

'Nine times out of ten,' agreed Knutter dutifully.

'Don't worry about it. You're a bit overwrought yourself, aren't you?'

Mark nodded. He was acutely conscious that he was making himself look ridiculous. There was no need to panic.

'I'm sorry,' he said humbly, 'but after what happened . . . '

Inspector Williams patted his shoulder comfortingly. 'After what happened we're naturally all concerned. Go along home and wait for her there. If she turns up and finds you gone we'll have both of you in a state. Let's find out *where* she's gone before we start jumping to conclusions.'

Mark forced a tight smile. Williams accompanied him as far as the door and ushered him out promising to keep in touch. He turned back to the two gentlemen waiting patiently to take their leave of him.

'Nothing to worry about,' he said cheerfully. 'A little domestic difficulty, I shouldn't wonder.'

★   ★   ★

The two gentlemen strolled along the side of the canal each apparently deep in his own thoughts. They paused at the lock gate where the path gave way to a muddied slushy track and idly stood watching a couple of boys trying to hit a floating can with little bits of stick and stones. The boys were so engrossed in their competition they did not seem to notice the presence of adults.

Across the road the lights of the small hotel winked back at them. Darkness was beginning to fall and the snow was coming down again, slowly descending flakes about the size of a penny spinning as they fell. Sellingby turned up his coat collar.

'So,' he said, interrupting his companion's contemplation of the black waters of the cut, 'it seems we will not be able to conclude our deal as quickly as we had hoped.'

'It's very inconvenient,' objected Harrap tetchily, 'to come all this way to see the woman and now she's not here.'

'Awkward of her,' Sellingby agreed. 'We must just make the best of the hospitality this provincial . . . ' he sniffed distastefully at the dark little streets and cobbled alleyways . . . 'posting offers us. Come now, Harrap. Make the best of things. For Queen and Country and all that.'

Harrap eyed the peeling front of the hotel, which was not much more than a large pub, with evident disgust.

'I'll put it down as five-star on my expenses,' he growled surlily.

'You do that.' Sellingby patted him on the shoulder and guided him across the road. The winking lights displayed two stars on the AA sign.

'We don't even know where the woman's gone,' Harrap protested, his voice almost sharpening to a whine.

'Indeed,' agreed Sellingby affably, 'but we'd better find out, hadn't we? Before anyone else does.'

★　★　★

Mark heard the knock on the door as a muffled thud rather than a conventional clack. At first it didn't register, then he remembered there was no letter box. He opened the door, with some difficulty as it was not properly rehung. Sergeant Knutter stood on the doorstep, his pale eyes faintly misty in the haze of the street lamp. Mark pulled the door open to let him in.

'I just called to see if you've heard anything, sir,' said Knutter, briskly pulling off his gloves. 'From your wife I mean.'

Mark shook his head. He indicated the open address book that he had left lying on what was left of the dining table, a rickety raft with splintered edges.

'I've tried everyone. No one's seen or heard from her.'

'She may have gone off by herself,' offered Knutter kindly. 'People do sometimes. Sometimes it helps to go off by yourself just to think things over.'

'She might have told me,' Mark pointed out in a spoiled little boy voice.

Knutter looked round at the debris-strewn room. Mark had made some attempt to tidy it up, and the wall was now firmly boarded, but it still looked a mess in anyone's eyes.

'Well, sir,' he said after a moment's pause, 'if we hear anything we'll let you know immediately. I shouldn't worry about it. No news is usually good news.'

Mark stared blindly at him as he went out. He looked around the rubbish filled room at the splintered and shattered furniture and the broken belongings, at the torn and shredded embroidered cushion sitting stupidly in the armchair. Don't worry?

He looked out the door and watched the bulky figure of the policeman with his swinging step disappear down the hill. The snow was falling thickly again like yards of net curtain discreetly obliterating the street. It had become quite dark and he hadn't noticed. The sodium yellow of the street lamp burned like a weak sun faintly gilding the pavement. He pulled the door shut. When the snow had eased off a bit he would get out the flashlight and go and look for her again . . .

# 11

'Where the hell is my wife?'

Edward Kelsey staggered back as the young man shoved past him into the house.

'How should I know . . . ? he began automatically.

Mark grabbed hold of him and manhandled him into the living-room where he bundled him violently on to the sofa.

'Where is she?'

Kelsey looked up at his towering adversary. He felt suddenly frail and rather old. Fear flickered momentarily in his dark eyes. Mark was tall, not powerfully built but stronger than he looked, and one thing was patently obvious — he was very, very angry.

'I've told you,' Kelsey said patiently, trying to keep his voice flat and calm. 'I don't know. Good God, man, don't you think I'm worried, too? I've had the police round here this morning and I could only tell them the same thing. I don't know where Lou is.'

Mark shot him a look of pure venom but the mention of the police seemed to have the desired effect. So they were taking the matter seriously after all. He threw himself into an armchair.

'What's she mixed up in?' he demanded bluntly. 'What the hell is she mixed up in, Kelsey?'

Edward Kelsey shook his head. 'I don't know, Mark. That's God's honest truth I swear to you. If I knew I'd tell you. All I know is that I thought she was . . . well frightened of something, or somebody.'

Mark was watching him with a stony look on his face. He still hadn't decided how good an actor this slippery little man was, the poor man's Robespierre. He was not himself a pretty sight. He hadn't shaved. He looked as if his head hadn't seen the pillow. His clothes were a mess.

'Frightened of what?'

Kelsey shrugged and sat forward on the settee placing his hands together as if in the act of prayer. He was beginning to recover his poise now.

'I've no idea. To tell the truth I thought she was frightened of you.'

'Of me?' Mark sat bolt upright. 'Why should she be frightened of me?'

Kelsey looked embarassed. 'I knew you'd had marital . . . troubles. Lou didn't go into details. She seemed reluctant to talk about it and I just formed my own suspicions.'

Mark sat forward in his chair and jabbed his finger belligerently in the air. 'Let me tell you something,' he said savagely, 'I may have an abominable temper. It's the Irish in me. I can't help that. I may have had my differences with her, but I will tell you this. I have *never* laid a finger on my wife in anger.'

Kelsey had the grace to look shame-faced. 'Sorry,' he said. 'As I said, I just jumped to conclusions.'

Mark leaned back in his chair satisfied that he had made his point. 'She had no reason to be frightened of me.'

Kelsey nodded as if he accepted this. 'Then I don't know what.'

'Or who?'

'Or who.'

Mark stood up and paced round the room. 'You *must* know,' he said desperately. 'You must know something. There's no one else. No one she would have confided in. Something's been going on. When the bomb went off you were there.'

'Coincidence surely?'

'She didn't want me to meet you.'

Kelsey's dark eyes flickered for a moment with something resembling a secretive smile. 'You have a jealous temper.'

'She's *disappeared*,' pointed out Mark emphatically, leaning menacingly over him, 'now what's the connection?'

This time the older man was not intimidated. He merely laughed.

'The Bolshevik connection you mean?'

'Why not?' Mark circled round him like a hungry tiger. 'Too many friends with foreign sounding names the old lady said.'

Kelsey looked up in surprise. 'What old lady?'

'Mrs . . . ' Mark reached for the name. 'Beedon, Brendon . . . something like that . . . no, Breedon.'

'Lily Breedon,' commented Kelsey with an understanding nod.

'You know her?'

He laughed again, a full throaty chuckle. 'You don't want to take too much notice of what she says. She's eighty-four, you know. Remarkable really but her mind's well . . . you know.'

He mimed a rocking movement with his hand.

Mark scowled at him. 'That's what she says.'

Kelsey's eyes danced with amusement. 'Man, she thinks a chap coming over from Sheffield is foreign. She's never moved out of this valley in her life.'

Mark sank back into his seat crestfallen. Mr. Kelsey let him subside for a while watching his anger ebb away and give way to the tiredness that was threatening to overwhelm him, then spoke gently.

'Of course it is possible that she's just trying to teach you a lesson,' he suggested.

'Teach me a lesson?' Mark echoed in disbelief.

'It is what you did to her, isn't it? Went off without a word? Maybe she's trying to get her own back. Give you a taste of your own medicine. That would be natural enough.'

'Just to disappear. Leave everything? Just like that?'

'Hell, they say, hath no fury like a woman scorned.'

'No.' Mark shook his head, 'Lou's not like that. Revenge isn't her style.'

Mr. Kelsey gave a little sideways inclination of the head which could have meant agreement or dissension. It was impossible to tell.

'You should know your own wife better than I do.'

Something in his tone drew a hot glance from Mark. 'Is this the Marriage Guidance Council again?'

'No, not at all,' Mr. Kelsey slapped his thighs to emphasise his point. 'I'm not a psychiatrist. I'm not saying it makes sense. If there's a man alive who claims to understand the workings of a woman's mind he's a liar in my opinion. I'm just offering a suggestion.'

'It's a possibility,' mused Mark. He sank back in the chair. The soft cushions seemed to swallow up his tired body. His eyes began to close in spite of his efforts to prevent them. 'But she didn't even pack.'

'Well, she wouldn't, would she?' observed Kelsey matter-of-factly. 'Not if she wanted to get you really worried.'

Mark's eyes were closed. Kelsey got up and went softly to the kitchen door.

'Where are you going?' Mark was not asleep yet. His eyes opened wide suddenly.

'Coffee,' Kelsey told him. 'You look like you could do with a gallon of it.'

Mark nodded. His eyes closed again.

'There's something going on,' he mumbled before he went to sleep, 'and I'm going to find out what it is.'

★ ★ ★

'It's very unfortunate about Mrs. McNamara,' said Mr. Sellingby softly, trying to catch the light filtering through the green blinds on the gold ring round his umbrella. 'Very unfortunate. I do think you should make every effort to find her.'

'We have dogs on the moors now, sir,' Inspector Williams told him briskly, 'but with the snow six feet deep in places it's going to be a long job.'

'What have you discovered so far?' inquired Sellingby in silky tones that betrayed no more than polite curiousity.

'Three dead sheep,' Williams informed him, consulting the file.

'*Dead* sheep? Dear, dear. Very unfortunate.'

'Unfortunate? Yes. Very.'

There was a little lull as Sellingby watched a fine beam of light like a laser cutting across the wall.

'When you do find Mrs. McNamara,' he went on suddenly, 'I think it would be advisable if you were to let me know first *before* you inform anyone else . . . before her husband even. For safety's sake.'

'Why is that, sir?' The policeman's expression was as politely vacant as the civil servant's. Both men were experts at wearing masks.

'Mrs. McNamara,' explained Sellingby evenly, 'used to work for INSOFT.'

Williams nodded in acquiescence. 'So her husband informed us.'

'We think she may be a ''connection'', he chose the word carefully, 'in our business.'

Williams stuck out his lower lip in a thoughtful bulldog face. 'Seems a reasonable assumption. Someone tried to rub her out, didn't they?'

Sellingby practised his Mona Lisa smile. '*Erase* is so much nicer,' he suggested facetiously.

The inspector's smile was more Cheshire Cat. 'Someone tried to *murder* her,' he amended.

'You haven't proved that.'

'An intelligent deduction. She was nearly blown to bits. She's a lucky lady.'

'Indeed. Another intelligent deduction.'

'We're good at those.'

'Even so,' purred Sellingby, 'we don't want it to happen again, do we?'

'Not on my patch,' retorted the policeman frankly. 'you don't really think she's in any danger from her husband, do you?'

Sellingby favoured him with another of his enigmatic smiles. 'Can't be too careful, can you?' he offered vaguely, as he glided from the room.

★ ★ ★

Lou woke to find herself blinking fiercely. A shaft of light was pouring its radiance directly into her face. She tossed from side to side to escape its intensity, then fully awakened by it, she sat up realising it was the sun cascading through an attic window that had caused her to stir into consciousness.

A sharp pain drove through the side of her head nearly making her cry out. It was a headache. She fell back against the soft pillow. Thank God, it was only a headache.

The walls of the room were yellow, a pale buttercup colour that soaked up the sun. They gave off a warm pleasant glow. The ceiling sloped sharply indicating the room was in the roof. The bed was under the shallowest part of it. The little pointed window was hung with cream net. The world outside was invisible.

There was a space for the bed, a tiny chest of drawers that did service as a bedside table, and an old-fashioned washstand with a big porcelain bowl and a matching jug decorated with brown and gold flowers. Lou admired it enviously. She would have given her eye teeth to get hold of one of those.

Pretty floral curtains decorated the windows and the same frilled material stuck out round the base of the washstand like a crinoline. The quilt was old-fashioned patchwork, American Colonial style.

Lou turned her head. A lampstand perched on the chest of drawers, a plaster shepherdess in a primrose dress holding up the shade with one hand and her crook in the other. There was no clock. She looked at her watch, shook her wrist and listened to it. It had stopped.

She had no idea how long she had been lying there. She tried to get up again but the pain stabbed in her head and she collapsed.

There was no sound outside the

window nor, it seemed from elsewhere in the house, until she heard a creak on the stairs and a heavy tread approaching.

The door opened. Sergeant Knutter squeezed his enormous frame through the small opening. He was carrying a cup of tea. He placed it on the chest of drawers.

'Well, Mrs. McNamara,' he said affably, perching himself on the end of the bed, 'all right are we?'

# 12

Ten days passed then there was a sudden change in the weather, one of those abrupt unpredictable changes that make it the principal topic of conversation and the British an incomprehensible wonder to other (in a meteorological sense) less volatile nations.

The snow melted. It vanished as silently as it had come leaving fast-flowing streams in the runnels and patches of wet bog on the hillside. The river rose almost to flood level and dashed through the valley in a gushing torrent, all white water. In place of the snow came heavy rain.

Sergeant Knutter and Mark walked slowly through the park. The branches dripped over their heads but they paid no mind to them. The riverbank was already beginning to crumble in some places where the water had risen to a dangerous level and the drains were overflowing producing small gurgling fountains of creamy, opaque fluid.

The park had that desolate look that belongs to wet playgrounds. The boarded up cricket pavilion and the deserted café offered no signs of welcome. There are few more miserable places on earth than a wet dale in winter.

'You've not heard anything then?' Knutter was asking as Mark dragged dejectedly by his side.

'Not a thing. I've kept ringing round and ringing round and no one can tell me anything.'

'We've heard nothing either,' said Knutter consolingly, 'Now the snow's gone the dogs have had a good chance to scour the moor and they've turned up nothing. That's a good sign.'

'Is it?' Mark paused to watch the rushing water carry away a dead branch dragging it down into the swirling currents. 'I keep thinking that she might be dead. I just can't get it out of my head.'

'You don't want to think like that sir,' urged Knutter cheerfully, 'nil desperandum. That's the ticket.'

'I can't sleep for thinking of it. Fearing the worst and the worst you can imagine, it . . . ' He couldn't put it into words, the nightmares, the sleeplessness — indeed the fear of sleep for the nightmares it might bring — the sick feeling that never left his stomach. He couldn't bring himself to say he felt broken.

Knutter looked at his gaunt, tired face and refrained from stating that it was obvious.

'Well, she's not on the moor, sir,' he said bluntly. 'I can tell you that.'

Mark nodded his gratitude. 'Well, that's something.'

They stopped as two boys came towards them. One, with his hands in his pockets had a cheeky roll in his step, an inborn swagger that went well with his frank, wide eyes and ginger curls. The other affected a studied nonchalance that sad oddly on his slight, childish frame.

'Found out who your man is yet?' the ginger one hailed Knutter boldly.

He shook his head. 'Not a thing. You turned anything up, have you?'

The boys looked a little sheepish. The

dark one shook his head in turn. 'Not while the snow's been about. Mam won't let us out. She's worried we'll get us feet wet.'

Knutter received this sympathetically. It was a problem faced by all investigators starting out in life.

'Oh, well,' he said philosophically as if a trifle disappointed they hadn't cracked the case for him, 'something'll come to light, never fear.'

The grown men strolled on leaving the boys to find their own amusement on the swings and roundabouts.

'I like kids,' offered the policeman by way of an explanation.

'Got any?'

'Two.'

Mark's surprised glance caught a gentle smile in response. Knutter knew perfectly well he did not look like the sort of man to dandle a baby on his knee, still less to have a devoted and attractive wife waiting for him at home. Appearances can be deceptive.

'Lou wants children,' said Mark flatly. He didn't say any more.

The two men left the park and crossed the railway bridge heading for the centre of town. Mark was disinclined to talk. The policeman seemed content with his own thoughts. They walked side by side but each in his way alone.

She was coming towards them. A long, dark coat of an indeterminate blue-black hid most of her, hanging nearly to her ankles, which disappeared into black suede bootees with a zip up the front. She wore a black velvet hat like a wrinkled prune square on her head, decorated a little off-centre with the eye of a peacock feather. A tartan muffler was crammed under her chin and she carried an enormous handbag in one gloved hand and in the other a rolled umbrella.

'Young man,' she said sharply, poking Mark with this instrument. He jumped, abruptly prodded out of his mind-wanderings.

'Hello, Mrs. Breedon,' he said wanly, remembering her name.

'Young man,' she said again sharply. 'You haven't been to see me.'

He shook his head apologetically. 'I've

been . . . preoccupied,' he said lamely.

'You promised you'd come and see me,' she retorted brusquely in the commanding tone that old ladies adopt when they are determined to get their own way.

'Yes, I know. Yes, I will come,' he promised vaguely.

'You'll come to tea?' It was more of an order than an invitation.

'Yes, thank you.'

'Tomorrow then. Four o'clock.'

She waved the brolly at him like a fairy godmother hoping to transform him into something rather more splendid than the dishevelled, dispirited creature that stood before her. 'You won't forget?'

Again it was a command rather than a question. He wasn't sure whether to nod or shake his head.

'I shall be expecting you so don't be late.' She parted the two men as Moses must have parted the Red Sea employing her umbrella as a staff.

'Oh, and young man,' she added as an afterthought, prodding him again, gently this time.

'Yes?' He looked at her with haunted eyes. The dark circles under them hung like half-moons down to the cheek-bones. Her haughty tone softened slightly.

'Do try and *shave* before you come.'

He nodded helplessly and watched her walk on, not altogether steady on her feet — she had to use her umbrella occasionally like a walking stick to support her — but sprightly considering. The last thing he noticed as she disappeared from sight was that absurd squashed prune clinging to her head.

*　*　*

Mark woke abruptly. He thought he heard a knocking at the door but it was only the ticking of the old clock in the kitchen. He had fallen asleep in the armchair. It was half-past three in the afternoon. He shook his head to see if anything stirred in his brain and rubbed his eyes. It was eleven days since Lou had disappeared. Eleven days and three hours. Eleven days of guilt mingled with grief and fear for her safety.

He remembered his appointment with the old woman. Four o'clock she had said, that gave him thirty minutes. He decided to go. He still hadn't written his article and he had a deadline to meet. The material would be useful if not riveting. It would, as people foolishly said at these times of personal torment, take him out of himself.

He went into the kitchen and stuck the kettle on the gas ring. The jets burst into flame with a whoosh at the flick of a match. He stared at the pale blue jets for a minute. They reminded him of the sky that morning when he had watched his wife making her way up the hillside.

He turned the gas off. He didn't want coffee after all. He gazed blankly round the room. What did he want? Shave, she said . . .

When Mrs. Breedon opened the door to him just before four she was agreeably surprised by his appearance. He had shaved and brushed his hair and his clothes were passably presentable although not very well ironed.

For her part she, too, had obviously

made an effort. Her tiny blue-grey curls had been lightly rollered and evenly distributed like a woolly cap. She wore a neat brown dress with a cream lace collar, broad with long points like that of a seventeenth century Puritan. A large amber brooch fixed at the centre of her neckline twinkled in the light of the streetlamp. It was late November and already beginning to get dark.

'Come in,' she said, in the sweet clipped tones of a hostess determined to play her part gracefully. He followed her inside.

The living room was a surprise. It was furnished with beautiful antique furniture, wax-polished and gleaming, reflecting the rich colours of the Persian-style Wilton carpet. An enormous dresser stood alongside the chimney breast loaded with china plates — Doulton, Minton, Meissen, with the odd piece of Crown Derby thrown in. Splendid silver jugs stood in a row along the mantelpiece. Mark could tell from their slightly dull shine they were not plated. Mrs. Breedon was obviously a collector with great taste.

In the centre of the room stood a small pedestal table loaded with the tea-tray. She had brought out the best bone-china in his honour. A roasting fire crackled in the grate. Eighty-four she might have been but she still knew the art of graceful living.

'I thought your husband was a union man.' Mark couldn't help remarking on the splendid contents of the room.

Mrs. Breedon smiled. 'He was indeed. Even when he became master of the Browndyke foundry he still kept his card and paid his dues. He was a sentimental man.'

'He owned it, you mean?'

'Eventually. I live in what you might call reduced circumstances,' admitted Mrs. Breedon sadly. 'It's no longer a family firm.'

Mark gazed round at her 'reduced circumstances'. 'I should think you must be very comfortable here.'

'I am,' she agreed. 'I don't want a large place. Not at my age. It's only the stairs that trouble me, but I don't want to move into one of those council places. Who wants to live with a lot of old people?'

Mark supressed a grin. She wasn't old, only 'getting on in years.'

'There's someone I want you to meet,' she told him, and going to the foot of the stairs called, 'You can come down now. He's here.'

Mark scarcely looked up as the third person clattered down the stairs into the room, then a glimpse of red hair caught his eye and his heart received a jolt.

He and Lou stared at each other. Her blue eyes seemed to penetrate his looking for some sign of reassurance but he could not read hers. They were clouded, guarded. She didn't speak. He was speechless.

'Why don't you sit down?' chimed in Mrs. Breedon merrily. 'Tea's for brewing, not stewing. Sit down, both of you.'

Stunned, Mark did as he was bidden, not knowing what to say. Mrs. Breedon gazed affectionately at them both in a motherly way.

'Well, this is nice, isn't it?' She lifted the china teapot and began to pour daintily.

Mark's gaze fell on a photograph that

stood on the dresser. It had caught his eye just before Lou entered the room. He reached out and lifted it down. It was a brown Victorian photograph in a gilt frame, an oval portrait in soft sepia of a plain woman with upswept hair.

'Do you know who that is?' asked Mrs. Breedon as if she were testing his general knowledge.

'Rosa Luxemburg.'

Her little bird-like eyes glittered. She was pleased by his answer.

'Yes. Rosa Luxemburg.'

He replaced the photograph with exaggerated nonchalance.

'The Bolshevik connection?'

Mrs. Breedon gave a little crackling laugh.

'More like the Methodist connection. Safe in the Arms of the Lord, my dear. Isn't that so, Louise? Much the best place to be.'

Lou said nothing. He tried to read some message in her eyes but she was still watching him with an anxious questioning stare. Were they still strangers in spite of their years together? What do we show of ourselves to anyone apart from the superficial gloss? She had dreams and aspirations. What had he cared about them apart from those in which he figured personally? She was his wife but he still couldn't read her mind.

Mrs. Breedon observed their uncertainty as if she sensed the barrier of mistrust between them. She stooped to stir the coals in the grate causing the yellow flames to flicker upwards like the tongues of buried serpents. Mark sat back casually in his chair and crossed his legs as if he were making himself at home.

'Well,' he said pleasantly, as if about to discuss the arrangements for the church fête, 'supposing you tell me which side you're on.'

Mrs. Breedon smiled her sweet smile and passed him a plate of macaroons.

'Now that,' she said honestly, 'is just what we were going to ask you.'

# 13

The attic room was quite dark. Lou switched the light on. It gave out a golden glow that spread over the coverlet but failed to dispel the furthest shadows in the room. There was hardly enough space for two. They both sat on the bed.

To her surprise he pulled her to him and covered her face with kisses. She drew back uncertainly.

'What was that for?'

'I thought you were dead.'

She shot him a wary look under her fringe of red gold hair that looped across her forehead and deliberately smoothed the edge of the sheet with her fingers.

'Did you care?'

'Care?' Mark stared at her. 'Of course I cared.'

'It's a fair question.'

She sat hunched up, withdrawn into herself. He touched her shoulder but she shrugged him off. He threw himself full length on the bed and lay on his stomach.

'All right,' he admitted after a short pause, 'it's a fair question. I guess I haven't shown myself the most devoted of husbands in the past. I suppose it's the old truism that you never realise how much you want something until you lose it, or think you've lost it. I've never felt so . . . desolate.' He turned over on his back and looked hard at her for a moment. 'Edward Kelsey says you ran out on me just to serve me a spiteful turn. Is that your game?'

She shook her head but it was no kind of answer. The gold in her hair gleamed like fine-spun metallic thread burnished by the soft light of the bedside lamp filtered through its vellum shade. He was stirred by tender feelings he had almost forgotten.

'Is that it, Lou?' he asked anxiously.

She shook her head again without looking at him but more definitely this time.

'No,' he said, reaching for her hand. This time she didn't draw it away. 'I didn't think that was all there was to it.

Not your style. I thought I knew you better than that. Are you going to tell me what it's all about?'

She hesitated. 'I still don't know.'

'Don't know what?'

'If I can trust you.'

It came out like a cry of pain, real anguish mingled with fear. She *was* afraid of him. He touched her cheek with a lover's gentleness.

'For Christ's sake, Lou. I'm your husband.'

She stared at him defiantly as if willing him to crack and take back that statement.

'I'm your *husband*,' he repeated emphatically. 'You can trust me. We have no secrets from each other, right?'

She gave him a dirty look. The words were not well chosen.

'Well, we shouldn't have,' he amended guiltily.

She heaved a deep sigh and lay back across him. He manoeuvred himself into a more comfortable position, freeing his left arm so he could stroke her hair. It was a little comforting gesture, an old habit designed to smooth away nightmares. She lay still for a moment letting the old magic work before making up her mind.

'It started about a year ago,' she explained, 'just before you left. I began to notice that some of the programs we were feeding in were curious. Usually you don't know what you're putting into the computer. It's a repetitive task, just feeding in figures. After a while it becomes mechanical but these were somehow curious.'

'What were they?'

'I didn't know at first. They didn't mean anything to me, just lists of figures — azimuths, elevations — it was all double Dutch to me. Anyway I mentioned it to a colleague — a Rhodesian, Geoff Randall, and he did know what they were.'

'How did he know?'

'He was a pilot. Ex-Rhodesian air force or something. He recognised that it was flight information of some kind. He checked it out. Mark, what we were sending out to Salisbury sandwiched between last month's bad debts and next week's invoices were the launch details for guided missiles.'

Mark clicked his tongue as if he were exasperated. 'He shouldn't have told you.'

'He had to.'

'He put you in danger. It wasn't necessary.'

'Yes, it was. I was the only one who had access to the tapes. A lot of the information we deal with is highly confidential. Security is very tight.'

'So you got the tapes for him?'

'Yes.'

'Why didn't you just report it?'

'We did. Not at once because we weren't sure who was behind it and Geoff reckoned it might be something big, so he got in touch with a friend of his at the MOD. He told me I shouldn't tell anyone about it. They'd made a list of possible suspects and they didn't want anyone to get wind of it in case they took off.'

'You stole the tapes?'

'I had to or they would have gone out to our Salisbury offices and we'd have lost track of them.'

'What did you do with them?'

She hesitated. 'I . . . I gave them to Geoff.'

'And he's dead now.'

She lowered her head sorrowfully and said in a small voice, 'Yes.'

'I suppose,' said Mark sarcastically, 'that he included your husband amongst the list of people you shouldn't speak to?'

She sat up and turned to face him, sweeping her hair off her face.

'I was going to tell you,' she confessed, 'but Geoff said I should wait until he'd checked it out with his friend at the Ministry of Defence.'

'And then what?'

She sighed as if the words cost her something to let go.

'Then he told me what kind of man you really are and now he's dead.'

'What does that mean?'

She looked him sharply straight in the face.

'Mark, you were top of the list.'

★   ★   ★'

London, sir?'

The detective sergeant looked up

absently from his desk where he was doodling on a blotter.

Mark nodded. 'I've just remembered some friends. They were friends of Louise really. I haven't seen them for a long time, but she might — she just might have gone to them. It's a chance, bit of a long shot really, but I have to try it.'

Sergeant Knutter nodded. 'Of course, sir. I understand Would you like to leave a forwarding address so we can let you know if she turns up here?'

Mark scribbled an address on a sheet of paper and handed it to him. 'If I'm not there they'll know where to reach me,' he explained. Knutter looked at the address thoughtfully but made no comment. He folded the scrap of paper carefully and slipped it into the desk drawer.

'London train leaves on the hour,' he offered helpfully.

Mark picked up his holdall. 'I'll be gone a day or two, I imagine.'

Knutter smiled. 'Any developments, sir, we'll let you know.'

As Mark left the office he passed Inspector Williams on his way in with

Sellingby and Harrap in tow.

'Where's he off to?' he asked his colleague with a jerk of the head over his right shoulder.

'London,' supplied the sergeant, scribbling another doodle on the pad.

'What for?'

'Business I should imagine, sir. Something to do with the paper he told me.'

'Funny time to go to London,' put in Sellingby, morally affronted, 'with his wife missing.'

'Well, sir,' said Sergeant Knutter realistically, picking up the bits and pieces he had left on the desk. 'It's been twelve days now. Lost on the moor. Blizzards. Freezing rain. Not much hope, sir.'

'You didn't tell him that?' protested Sellingby shocked.

'Oh, no, sir. We always like to hold out a little ray of hope. That's between ourselves of course.'

'You haven't found anything then?' Sellingby was the curious bystander once more.

Inspector Williams shook his head and slid into the chair Knutter had vacated for him.

'There are deep bogs on the moor. If she fell into one of them we'd never find the body,' he pointed out.

'You think that's what happened to her?' Sellingby questioned him earnestly.

'That's the way she was heading.'

'Poor man.'

'Not much joy for you either, sir.'

'For me?'

'You can't question her. About your business.'

'No,' Sellingby delicately smoothed his eyebrows. 'It looks like a wasted journey. I said that this morning to Harrap. Didn't I, Harrap?'

Harrap responded by looking glum.

'You'll be going back to London, too, then, sir?' suggested Knutter airily.

Sellingby half-smiled, the neither for you nor against you non-committal expression of the perfect public servant. 'All in good time,' he suggested pointedly. 'Something may yet turn up.'

Knutter was satisfied. With some people you always felt happier when you could keep an eye on them.

# 14

According to the vagaries of the islands' climate London had not seen any snow. When Mark stepped down from the train on to the platform at Euston Station he felt the temperature had risen markedly. It had not. He had just travelled south.

The station concourse, a vast modern hall with its shining tiled floor and walls of glass, was crowded as usual, the long-distance travellers burdened with overfilled suitcases and assorted zipper bags confused with the regular commuters involved in the daily dash from British rail to underground, an unstoppable stream of the bored and withdrawn, finding their way by sixth sense alone, since all other senses are temporarily suspended during the regular monotonous passage from home to office, like so many ants scurrying blindly through the maze of tunnels and escalators.

Mark didn't make for the underground

— the usual route across the city. Fleet Street was not his destination. He weaved his way through the concourse and passed through the glass doors into the station forecourt, through an elegant concrete square with a black fountain like a surrealist screw left over after the construction of the complex, and into the Euston Road, three lanes of busy traffic in both directions.

He crossed at the traffic lights taking his life in his hands for they were designed to promote the unceasing flow of vehicles and took no account of pedestrians. He turned right along the Euston Road and then left by Dillons, the 'university bookshop' as it proudly proclaimed itself.

He cast a perfunctory glance in the bookshop windows as he passed. They were doing a nice line in ergonomics but he was not tempted to stop and browse. He went on up the street, past the union where bunches of bored looking students sat staring out of the window at the occasional passer-by. A group of them passed him cheerfully, laughing and joking, followed by a disgruntled lecturer, no doubt conscious that his spirited attempt to cram their minds with 'Locke and the Liberty of England — the 17th century dream' had failed to make any noticeable impression.

He went on walking past the impressive Gothic college buildings, conceived in a day when academic interests went hand in hand with the ecclesiastical resulting in these cathedral-style buildings, into Gordon Square. Here tall, elegant houses formed three sides of the square in the centre of which a pleasant garden was laid out and protected from the public by iron railings. This barrier had the effect of creating a sanctuary, a haven of peace in the heart of a busy city. The growl of traffic around Byng Place did not seem to penetrate the railings. The green unruffled lawns remained invitingly inviolate. Once it had been a social gathering place where the residents could take the air but there were few genuine residents now. Most of the houses had been turned over to offices. It was preserved largely as a pleasant reminder of what the city's glass and concrete had progressively overtaken.

Mark strolled along two sides of the square then halted in front of one of the tall white houses in the terrace. This was the one he was looking for. It had a black shiny front door newly painted.

He stepped into the porch and consulted the name-plates affixed to the doorpost. They were small, brass rectangles neatly engraved and positioned one exactly above the other. Their pristine condition — together with the new paintwork suggested that the companies had not been in residence long.

The first one relating to the top floor read '*Christie-Bellamy (Consultants) Ltd*', the second '*Christie-Bellamy (Carriers) Ltd*', and occupying the ground floor '*Christie-Bellamy (Communications) Ltd.*' He pressed the bell alongside the top plate marked '*Christie-Bellamy (Consultants) Ltd*' and waited.

Here a short digression is required.

The most commonly used medium for the transmission of computer data both nationally and internationally is the telephone system. Links are established by dialling on the Post Office switched public network or by leasing lines from the Post Office and international 'carriers', that is by companies providing a private system of telecommunications. Telephone channels for long-distance transmissions are grouped together in this case in carrier systems using coaxial cable, microwave or satellite links. The preference for private carriers of this kind rather than the normal telephone links is quite simply explained. The telephone network is designed for voice transmission but channels giving the most acceptable voice quality cause serious distortion of the waves used for serial data transmission which leads to errors in the data received. Private carriers are able to provide leased lines that have been equalised to reduce the distortion to some extent and are thus able to offer better quality transmission.

The extraordinarily rapid growth of this section of the telecommunications industry has caused a number of problems for Her Majesty's and other foreign governments. The transmission of data at high speed by private companies via direct links abroad means that it is possible to transmit highly confidential information in a way that makes its passage out of the country almost undetectable. Every citizen is becoming aware of the danger to individual privacy caused by the growth of computer technology and its use by credit control companies and powerful bureaucracies. Imagine that writ large.

The company known as Christie-Bellamy (Carriers) Ltd is one of the largest of the private international carriers in the telecommunications field. It is a fact, of which the majority of tax-payers are probably unaware because such transactions are tucked away in the small print of obscure white papers read only when the House is asleep or for the most part absent, that HMG are the principal shareholders in this company, as they are in a number of other key firms which are not normally thought of as being nationalised. The combined concern of the Home Office, MOD and Foreign

Office is by no means the product of the peculiar insularity that grips the British administration from time to time. The industry itself is beginning to be aware that in releasing its exciting burst of technological development it has unleashed a force beyond its immediate control that may one day have as profound an effect on the balance of international affairs as the atomic bomb.

These growing fears are embodied in the CCITT[1], an international body belonging to the United Nations organisation the 'International Telecommunications Union' set up to introduce international standards to govern the world-wide flow of information.

The possibility of fast, virtually undetectable international communications poses threats both in terms of its possible use by organized and specialized crime — the potential for fraud on a grand scale is massive — and the fragile web of national security that protect the member

---

[1] *Comité Consultatif International de Télégraphie et Telephonie*

states of the UN from each other, that require a hard, professional, expert approach to the problems it produces. Accordingly a short while ago a subsidiary company to Christie-Bellamy (Carriers) Ltd (again with HMG as a principal shareholder) was set up — Christie-Bellamy (Consultants) Ltd — under the unpublicised auspices in the international field of the CCITT, with a view to investigating the vulnerability both of national defence systems and the world money-markets as they are weakened by the spread of on-line computing.

★  ★  ★

Mark waited for a response to his summons. There was a small speaker set into the wall beside the door such as one finds in more superior blocks of flats. After a moment this crackled slightly and a gritty female voice demanded 'Yes?'

'McNamara,' he said.

'Password?'

'Stuff it, Zoo. Let me in. I'm in a hurry.'

There was a slight tapping sound as if

someone were drumming a pencil close to the microphone.

'Password?' repeated the gritty voice irritably.

'Up Yours.'

There was a sharp intake of breath and an even sharper click as the microphone was switched off. Mark waited then pushed against the door. It swung open. He grinned to himself and ran up the stairs two at a time. Victory was always sweet. At the top of the stairs were double doors marking the entrance to the suite of offices. He pushed through these and went it.

Zoo was glaring at him. She was a short, middle-aged woman with dark-grey hair and a leathery complexion. Her father optimistically had christened her Zuleika after Max Beerbohm's famous Miss Dobson but she had failed to live up to the fabled beauty of her namesake. She was a solid, hearty sort of woman redolent of hockey and Angela Brazil. She even spoke in the curious clipped upper class tones that one nowadays hears only in British movies.

'Procedure,' she rapped furiously, 'you might observe procedure. That's what it's there for. To be observed.'

He did not bother to argue the absurdity of this argument. It was in any case pointless since with Zoo it was a religious belief. He merely planted a kiss on her forehead. 'Procedure observed,' he declared arrogantly. 'Is it all right to go in?'

'No,' she said, but he had already gone.

The office he walked into was a long rectangular room, half-panelled with dark oak. At the far end a long window looked out on to the green square. It was hung with darker green curtains. The carpet likewise was green. A long polished table dominated, occupying most of the floor-space and running nearly the length of the room. It was a conference table flanked by high-backed chairs. At the far end, since the room doubled as conference room and office, a desk was placed crosswise to the table making a giant T-shape. Behind the desk sat Rufford.

He was a big man, not just large but so enormous he seemed to have squeezed himself with some difficulty into his chair which was designed to hold a reasonably well-built adult with comfort. He was not an old man, forty to forty-five being a reasonable guess, and his muscular development indicated that he was physically in exceptional shape. He had once played at prop for the British Lions. His face looked as if it had been stamped on as indeed it had. The nose, broken on more than one occasion and in more than one place, undulated across his face and splayed out dramatically at the tip. The cheeks were decorated with scars like fine engraving. His hairline was receding so the whole richly contoured map was topped only by a fine fuzz of blond curls. He had nice hazel eyes, but otherwise no one could say he was a pretty fellow.

His desk was awash with files and papers but when Mark walked in he didn't seem to be studying any of them. He was making odd gestures with his pencil as if he were casting a line for fish.

'Catch anything?' asked Mark cheekily, catching him in the act. Looking a trifle sheepish Rufford made as if to write something down.

'Have you?' he retorted sternly. 'That's more to the point. Zoo?' he added looking towards the door where his secretary was standing arms akimbo in silent protest. 'Do you think you could manage two cups of coffee, please?'

'Certainly,' she said obediently, closing the door behind her.

'Soul of discretion Zoo,' commented Rufford affectionately.

'In that case,' objected Mark, 'how come she knows everything that's going on?'

Rufford smiled wryly. 'Did you make contact with Randall?'

Mark shook his head. 'Unfortunately by the time I got there he'd passed on.'

'Passed on to where?'

'Shuffled off this mortal coil or whatever the expression is.'

'Bloody hell!'

'I thought you'd have heard. The MOD know. They identified him.'

'The MOD?'

'They've got a couple of men up there.'

Zoo came in with the coffee. She kept

it permanently on the boil. She placed one cup carefully in front of Rufford, clearing a little space on the desk so it wouldn't spoil his papers, then banged the other hard down in front of Mark so that the contents slopped in the saucer.

'So kind,' he murmured gratefully.

She gave him an evil look and stalked out.

'You've upset her,' observed Rufford calmly. 'You should have observed procedure.'

'She's so bossy,' objected Mark pettishly.

'She is,' Rufford sighed. 'All secretaries are. The power they wield is enormous yet here we have modern women complaining that we don't take enough notice of them.'

'I didn't come to discuss the emancipation of the serfs.'

'Of course not.' Rufford daintly tapped a couple of saccharin into his cup. 'Of course Zoo's exceptional. It comes from having grown up in Africa. All those years of treating the natives like dirt.'

'I didn't know there would be an MOD

man involved,' Mark interrupted him, sticking to the subject.

Rufford sighed again. He had something of the mournful grandeur of a very old bloodhound. 'Almost inevitable, I'm afraid. Empire building. Nobody minds treading on anybody's toes these days. No courtesy between departmental heads at all. What's the name?'

'Sellingby.'

'Department?'

'God knows. Sounds like the extra ingredient you put in to get the brighter, whiter wash.'

'They've changed them all again so it doesn't matter. They all move one office down the corridor while the end one's being painted and they change the whole bloody departmental nomenclature . . . Is that the word . . . nomenclature? No wonder the post never finds them.'

'Is that what they tell you?'

'Perrenial excuse, dear boy. Sellingby and whose army?'

'Harrap. EDS, Ltd.'

'And poor old Geoff Randall's snuffed it.' Rufford's face crumpled again like a piece of newspaper. 'What exactly did you come down for?'

Mark gestured wildly. 'Answers.'

Rufford took up his pencil. 'All right then. Give me the questions.'

'Sellingby and Harrap. How much do they know about our operation? I mean, should we co-operate with them or not?'

'Not,' was the decisive reply. 'They'll only ball it up.'

'Edward Kelsey and the Bolshevik connection, if there is one. Are they involved or am I just getting paranoid?'

'I'll check it out.'

'Who's got the tapes now? My wife says she gave them to Randall. If so, where are they now? The police claim they found nothing on him.'

'Nothing?'

'Clean as a whistle.'

'Curious,' commented his boss.

'Can I believe a word my wife tells me?'

Something in Mark's tone caused Rufford to look up. 'Only you can judge that,' he said wisely.

'You knew she was involved?'

'So Randall gave me to understand.'

'You didn't see fit to tell me?'

'I thought it would be better if you weren't involved. You were rather tied up when this thing came up.'

'I'm involved now.'

'Yes,' was all Rufford's comment.

'You've no objection?'

'Can't be helped. I've got no one else.'

'One more thing,' added Mark after a moment's pause. 'According to Lou, Geoff Randall had me down as his chief suspect. Who do you suppose gave him that idea?'

Rufford looked thoughtful. 'Someone doesn't want you involved?'

'Looks like it, doesn't it?'

'I suppose it was reasonable. Trust no one that's the motto in our game.'

'It wasn't you?'

The big man shook his head. 'Not this time. As I said you were otherwise engaged. Unless of course he had reasonable grounds for suspicion.'

'Such as?'

'Accessibility. You worked for INSOFT before I took you on.'

'You trusted me.'

Rufford beamed benevolently. 'I'm just a big softie.'

'If you didn't make Randall suspicious who did?'

'I'll make a note of it.'

'Do you still trust me?'

'Innocent till proven guilty.'

'Thanks a lot.'

'Don't mention it.'

'Anyway,' concluded Mark sounding very disgruntled, 'It didn't do Randall any good.'

'What didn't?'

'Trusting no one. He's still dead.'

Rufford's gaze flickered over the list he had compiled. 'Gosh, what a lot of questions! Well, we'd better see what information we can give you.' He flicked the switch of the intercom. 'Zoo?'

Back came the gritty reply. 'Yes?'

'What have we got Xanadu filed under?'

There was a slight pause then back came the sharp response. 'Try X.'

# 15

The blue light burst through the night, whirling slowly up the hill like the tail-light of a low-flying UFO. Above it a million stars twinkled like diamanté sprinkled on velvet. The topaz glow of the street-lamps strung together by threads of radiance like a rosary completed the jewel-like image of the night sky. The blue light dipped out of sight momentarily then reappeared accompanied this time by a monotonous two-tone siren. It was an ambulance.

Mark trudged up the hill in its wake conscious only of his own aching tiredness. The London train had been two hours late owing, they said, to a points failure and he had been obliged to stand all the way in an overcrowded carriage. From the crown of the little humped-back bridge the road sloped away again and then, he thought with relief, it would be downhill all the way into the town. He could have got a taxi at the station but there were none about and to wait for one meant more standing about so he had decided to walk and stretch his long legs. Now he was regretting it.

As he followed the path the ambulance had taken down towards the river he noticed a small crowd of people gathered in the street. The ambulance had stopped, its doors flung wide open and the attendants were carrying a folded stretcher into the house. There was a police car parked across the road, hazard lights flashing. Mark hesitated for a second then started to run.

As he reached the knot of people the ambulance men were closing the doors on their patient and climbing into the cab. Mark grabbed the arm of one of the watching neighbours.

'What's happened?' he demanded abruptly.

'It's Mrs. Breedon,' said the woman in shocked tones.

'Is she ill?'

'Dead.'

Mark felt as if he'd been rocked back

on his heels by a physical blow. It was not possible.

'Dead?' he echoed foolishly as if he didn't understand what she meant by the word. 'Dead?'

The woman nodded. 'What is the world coming to?' she said with a deep sorrowful sigh.

'Thugs, that's what they are,' interrupted a small, grey-haired woman aggressively. 'Evil people, that's what they are. There's no excuse for them so don't tell me there is.'

Mark wasn't going to. 'They?' he demanded sharply. 'Who are 'they'?'

'Kids they said,' explained the first woman in soft sympathetic tones. 'How could they do it? I just don't understand it. She was just a dear old lady. I don't suppose she had anything much worth stealing.'

Mark thought of her magnificent silver and collection of antiques but it was not their loss that concerned him. All that kept flashing through his mind at that moment was the thought 'There was only one stretcher.'

'She was alone in the house then?' he asked, trying to sound a curious but not interested party.

The soft-spoken woman nodded sorrowfully. 'That's the terrible part about it,' she said almost in a whisper. 'We were next door and didn't hear a thing. Dad likes the television on loud you see.'

Mark nodded in an understanding way but couldn't help asking, 'There was only one body then?'

She looked at him, faintly surprised, as if to say one was more than enough.

'Oh, yes,' she said definitely. 'She was alone in the house.'

Mark heaved a sigh of relief which she took for regret. They waited as the police made the house secure, despatched the ambulance moaning through the darkness, its blue light sweeping in regular circles, and began clearing the street, then they drifted away. Mark drifted as far as the alleyway then slid round the back of the house. He had to know if Lou was safe.

He had difficulty finding his way without a torch or other light to guide him. He tripped over a dustbin and waited with bated breath for the clatter to die down. He heard a man's voice nearby exclaim 'Bloody cats!' and hesitated, wondering if he would come and investigate but he was not tempted from his fireside and Mark moved gingerly on, feeling his way along the wall that enclosed the narrow gardens. He found the back gate to Mrs. Breedon's property and let himself quietly into her garden. It was easy to see how the burglars had gained entry to her house. The kitchen window had been broken. This was now covered by a piece of cardboard as a temporary measure until it could be reglazed. Mark inspected it. It was only held in place by sellotape. He carefully removed it, slid his arm through the jagged hole and unlocked the back door, then he crept through into the dark kitchen.

Once in the house he abandoned secrecy and switched on the light, deeming it safer than bumping into the furniture which might bring the neighbours running in. The kitchen and living

185

room were as usual, spick and span. He looked around for a sign of the struggle. There was none. He was puzzled. The room looked exactly as it had, the plates on the dresser, the gleaming silver on the mantelpiece. He had read of old ladies being beaten and robbed of pathetically small amounts, mindless thuggery was the current national disgrace, but surely no burglar would be so amateur as to leave such obvious treasures unrifled? Only the portrait of Rosa Luxemburg was missing from the dresser.

'Lou?' he called quietly, going to the foot of the stairs. The house was deathly quiet. He could hear the muffled burbling of next door's television through the walls, perhaps, he reflected grimly, reporting the event they had missed. His footsteps creaked loudly on the stairs, but he was confident they would not hear him.

'Lou?' he called a little louder.

The bedroom door stood open. Everything was neat therein. Only the squashed prune hat sitting oddly on the bed like a crinkled cat suggested that someone had left the room unprepared. It seemed to act like a catalyst on him.

'Lou?' he shouted suddenly, discarding all pretence to stealth, 'Lou, where are you?'

He ran up the last flight of stairs three at a time and burst into the attic room. It was empty. She was not there. He sank on to the bed and buried his head in his hands.

'Christ,' he said aloud to himself, 'What now?'

# 16

A wedge of light squeezed its way through the narrow, barred window and diffused itself in diagonal lines like a Chinese fan painting a yellow triangle on the dirty white walls. The walls were brick, the floor concrete, the door thick, black steel.

Lou shifted her position on the bed. She felt as if she were sitting under a spotlight and the feeling made her uncomfortable. She shrank back into the corner where the shadows still gathered untouched by the warm glow of the penetrating sunlight and watched the dust dance in the beams that probed the farthest corners of the room.

The bed creaked ominously as she moved. It was metal-framed and sprung. The mattress was lumpy. She had spread the patchwork quilt across it to make the place look more like home. Beside the bed stood a dark green metal locker on top of which the plaster shepherdess spreading her skirts daintily held her lamp aloft. In the circle of her light sat a small bowl of anenomes. In addition to the bed and the locker the cell was furnished with a padded garden chair with brightly upholstered floral cushions and a striped Indian durry covered part of the cold floor. Every effort had been made to brighten up the room and make it cheerful but it still retained its customary air of gloom.

Lou leaned back against the wall and counted her blessings. They didn't seem to amount to much. She longed to get out of this dismal basement but it was the only place she felt really safe. What had her life come to, she reflected bitterly, when she felt safe only hunched in the shadows of a locked room?

She wondered how long she would have to stay like this. How long would her incarceration be necessary? If she left this sanctuary where could she go? Who could she trust?

She thought of Mark and wondered where he was at that moment. In her heart she longed to trust him but her common sense warned her to be wary. Why had he turned up just at this time? Why had he disappeared shortly after Geoff Randall had warned her against him? Was if just because she had become withdrawn from him? Had her mistrust destroyed their marriage and hastened his disillusion? It was a possibility. She prayed that it was so. His presence in the town had been a coincidence, nothing more. He had said so. Coincidences *did* happen. He had told her to trust him because he was her husband. She had trusted him enough to marry him. Shouldn't she take his word now before another's?

She had done a lot of praying lately. She had prayed desperately for a sign to guide her. It was so difficult to tell the good guys from the bad these days. Maybe there really was nothing to choose between them anymore. In the old days it was obvious from the way they wore their hats. A hat said it all — a deep brimmed fedora that hid the face in shadow, a cheeky trilby, smart bowler, a rakish boater or panama — the hat said it all, an instant character reading. No one wore hats anymore.

Which should she allow to rule her judgement — heart or head? It was a difficult decision to make. Love that could not be trusted was worth nothing and she was not anxious to dismiss something that had filled an important gap in her life lightly, however much it had been the cause of bitterness in the past. Cast adrift as she was she felt she had to cling on to something. On the other hand she was not a fool. She shook her head in despair. She couldn't decide. Neither was infallible.

There was a knock at the door, a hollow reverberating knock, like the summons of Doom, she thought melodramatically.

'Come in,' she called.

Inspector Williams entered bearing two mugs of tea.

'I thought you might like a bit of company for a while,' he offered cheerfully, handing her one of the mugs, a white one with a beaming hippopotamus painted in pink on the side, 'and I've got a few things to ask you. You don't mind?'

Lou shook her head and motioned him to sit down. He pulled the garden chair round to face her and wedged himself into it.

'What about Mrs. Breedon?' she asked wanly, sipping the strong tea.

Inspector Williams made himself comfortable. 'She's fine. She rang us from Weston-Super-Mare. She's having a whale of a time.'

'She was very kind.'

'Yes. Funny old dear. Heart of gold.' The policeman leaned forward slightly to appear a little more business-like and asked gently, 'Geoff Randall. What happened the night he died, Mrs. McNamara? Did you see him?'

Lou took a deep breath and nodded. 'He came to my house. He was very worried.'

'Was he ill?'

Lou looked startled. It was not the question she had been expecting. She hesitated. 'He had a cold. I told him to stay. It was a very cold night. Frosty. I thought he had the flu. He was running a high temperature. He seemed a bit feverish, but he wasn't really ill. Not with anything he might die from.'

'But he wasn't feeling well?'

'No. You know how you feel with the flu. Pretty rotten.'

'You feel worse than you are?'

'That's what he said.' Lou unconsciously smoothed her hair as she was thinking. 'But he was afraid.'

'Of what?'

'He thought someone was trying to murder him.'

'Following him?'

'Yes . . . well, no . . . I'm not really sure. I don't think he was. He seemed confused but he had this idea in his head. He was on the run. That's why he wouldn't stay. He couldn't sit still.'

'Perhaps he knew,' mused Williams thoughtfully. 'A sort of sixth sense. He may have had some idea what was happening to him.'

'What?' Lou's eyes widened.

'He was being poisoned.'

'Poisoned?'

'Did you give him anything?'

Lou looked frightened. 'Only one of those cold-cure powders. For the flu. It wouldn't have poisoned him. He had nothing else. I offered him supper but he wouldn't stay.'

'It's unlikely anything you gave him poisoned him,' the inspector pointed out reassuringly. 'The substance must have been in his system for some time. He died soon after leaving you.'

'Then why did you ask?' retorted Lou belligerently in response to what she saw as a hidden accusation.

'Just for the record,' he replied mildly. 'It helps to have all the facts.'

'Yes. I suppose so.' Lou let her fear subside. The inspector gave her a moment to compose herself.

'What time did he leave?'

'About eight.'

'Which way did he go?'

'The back way, across the heath.'

'Why did he go that way?'

'He didn't want anyone to see him arrive or leave. He didn't want them — '

'Them?'

'Whoever might be following him, if

anyone was — he didn't want to lead them to me. As I said, he was scared.'

'Did he scare easily?'

'I shouldn't think so. He was a pilot. R.A.F. man.'

'So you took him seriously?'

'Of course.'

The inspector examined the ends of his fingers closely then pressed them purposefully together before asking his next question.

'Why did he want to see you, Mrs. McNamara?'

Lou corrected him. 'He didn't want to see me.'

The policeman's brow contracted into a puzzled frown.

'Not you?'

Lou shook her head. 'I thought it was strange.' she admitted.

'Who *did* he want to see?'

'My husband.'

'Your *husband*?' The policeman's expression showed he was becoming increasingly perplexed. 'Why would he want to see your husband?'

'Mark used to work for INSOFT. He

left just after Geoff joined the firm. Geoff didn't know we'd split up permanently. He expected to find Mark with me.'

Inspector Williams whistled. 'Curiouser and curiouser,' he remarked ironically. 'I thought your husband didn't know anything about computers.'

'Mark?' Lou sounded surprised. 'He's an expert. He's one of the most brilliant software designers in the country.'

'Is he now?' responded the policeman drily. 'I wonder why he told that fib.'

'He's given it up now. He said it was driving him round the bend. It can cause nervous breakdowns. I've known it happen to a few people.'

'But you were the one who stole the tapes?'

Lou nodded guiltily.

'Then why would Geoff Randall want to see your husband?'

Lou shrugged. 'I don't understand. Geoff told me not to tell Mark anything about it.'

'He thought he might be implicated.'

'He wasn't sure. He was being cautious.'

'But on the night he died he wanted to see him?'

'Yes. He wanted to give him the tapes.'

'To your husband?'

'Yes.'

'Not to you?'

'No. He said Mark would know what to do with them.'

Inspector Williams sat back and considered the evidence. 'He must have found out something that changed his mind. Something that put your husband on the side of the angels.'

Lou's eyes brightened hopefully. 'Do you think so?'

'Makes sense. All the same,' he added cautiously, 'I'm not taking any chances. I don't want him to know where you are until I'm sure. Understand?'

Lou nodded. 'But I can tell him I'm all right?'

'Oh, yes. Did Randall have the tapes on him?'

'Yes.'

'We didn't find them on him. What did he do with them?'

Lou hesitated. 'He gave them to me.'

'I see.'

The young Inspector took her empty mug from her and asked gently, 'Would you like to tell me what you've done with them, Mrs. McNamara?'

Lou eyed him warily. He seemed a nice young man, stockily-built, broad-shouldered, dependable. He had a round, youthful face and humourous grey eyes. He reminded her in a way of Geoff Randall. She had told Geoff Randall her secret and now he was dead. The young policeman watched her placidly. After a moment or two's consideration she shook her head. 'I think I'd better wait till my husband gets back,' she said.

He didn't press her. He simply nodded as if this was fair enough. 'Well,' he observed, looking distastefully round the grubby room, 'I'm sorry we can't make you more comfortable. It's hardly four-star accommodation but at least you're safe here. No one's going to think of looking for you in the police station. Is there anything you need? Anything we can get you?'

She smiled and ran her fingers through

her fringe. 'I'd like to wash my hair.'

He grinned. 'Of course. I'll get one of the W.P.C.s to fix things up for you.'

He went out and the cell door banged shut behind him.

★　★　★

The telephone rang as soon as Mark entered the house. He picked up the receiver as he kicked the door shut and answered it, tucking it under his chin so he could pull his coat off at the same time. It was Rufford.

'Mark?'

'Yes?'

'Poor old Geoff was poisoned.' Rufford sounded as if he took this irregularity as a personal affront.

'Did you find out how?'

'Bit of a mystery, dear boy. Endless possibilities. Sort of atropine apparently. Very toxic.'

'Atropine?'

'African deadly nightshade or whatever they call it there. Sort of stuff Bushmen tip their arrows with. Kills a small antelope in no time.'

'Charming.'

'Quite painless I'm told.'

'Small comfort.'

'My sentiments exactly.'

There was a pause then Rufford continued. 'I've got something to tell you.'

Mark was all eager attention. 'I'm listening.'

'Not over the phone. It's a bit personal. You could have a crossed line. Don't want all the neighbours to know. Not something we want to get around. I'm coming up.'

'When?'

'Tomorrow. Train arrives 1800 hours. Zoo says that's six o'clock to you.'

Mark laughed. 'Six o'clock. All right. I'll be there.'

'Good. Oh . . . and Mark?'

'Yes?'

'Stay away from it there's a good lad.'

'What?'

'Deadly nightshade. Remember I'm short-staffed.'

'Yessir,' said Mark smartly and Rufford hung up.

# 17

The police station in Ravenhill was a four-storey, rectangular building of red brick in the eighteenth century style with long sash windows. It reposed at the end of the aptly-named 'Shady Lane'. Whether this was a local joke or meant to refer to the presently leafless plane trees that lined the narrow road Mark didn't know. The front door of the police station was reached by means of a high stoop flanked on either side by a low wall. The basement was lit by narrow barred windows at street level. Mark presumed these gave into the cells. On the end of the left hand wall stood a twisted pillar which caught the eye. It was of black cast-iron and supported a very old and very distinctive blue lamp.

The reception area was light and airy served by two of the huge windows which must have been nine or ten feet tall. It was separated from the porch by a polished swing door set with small panes of glass. Mark pushed this open and went to the counter where a pretty young W.P.C. was tackling the filing.

'My name's McNamara,' he said. 'I've come to see if there's any news about my wife.'

The young woman smiled sympathetically.

'Just one moment, sir,' she said kindly. 'I'll go and check for you.'

Mark waited. He looked round. Coloured posters decorated the walls — mostly warnings about road safety and watching out because there's a thief about. The occasional wanted poster portrayed a sullen, seedy-looking individual in stark black and white, occasionally in a variety of disguises. They were all wanted for crimes with violence — terrorist attacks, shotgun raids, rape and murder. A sign of the times, thought Mark glumly.

Opposite the counter ran a row of green chairs, backs to the wall. On one of these sat Mr. Sellingby, very straight, his document wallet balanced across his knees, resting his hands on the crook of his umbrella. In spite of his stiff posture he seemed perfectly at ease.

'You've not heard anything?' he inquired, pleasantly curious.

Mark looked at him. 'Heard anything?'

'About your wife. You haven't located her yet?'

Mark shot him a look of deep suspicion. What business was it of his? 'Not yet.'

Mr. Sellingby clicked his tongue against his teeth, whether in irritation or sympathy it was difficult to tell.

'It must be a very worrying time for you,' he offered dutifully.

'Yes,' snapped Mark shortly, disinclined to discuss his private affairs.

'One hears of so many terrible things happening nowadays,' murmured Mr. Sellingby softly, waving his hand over the catalogue of crime that was pinned to the noticeboards.

Mark glared savagely at him. Mr. Sellingby faltered. 'I didn't mean to suggest . . . '

'Then don't.'

'One wouldn't want to think anything *unpleasant* might befall your wife. That's what I meant to say. One hopes she has simply . . . wandered. Amnesia perhaps.'

'Perhaps.'

Mark felt faintly uneasy in this man's company. What did Sellingby know about his wife's disappearance? He recalled that he had been present when he burst into the station to report her missing. He was probably just idly curious to know the outcome. Mark shook the thought from his mind. There was no point in tilting at shadows. He was beginning to jump at every rustle.

The W.P.C. came back with Sergeant Knutter, whose solid bulk seemed to anchor the whole business firmly in reality.

'Good morning, sir,' he said breezily. 'How did your business go?'

'Business?'

'In London.'

Mark hunched his shoulders in an indifferent shrug. 'So-so.'

'It was worth the trip though?'

'Can't say just at the moment. Any news?'

'I'm afraid not, sir. As we were more or less. We'll let you know as soon as we hear anything definite.'

Mark sighed like a man resigned to bad fortune. 'I just thought I'd call in and let you know I've returned.'

Sergeant Knutter smiled appreciatively. 'Yes, sir. Thank you. We'll know where to find you if there is any news.'

Mark turned dejectedly away. As he pushed through the door he heard Sergeant Knutter say, 'Mr. Sellingby? The Inspector will see you now.'

So Sellingby was working with the police for his part in the investigation. He was on the side of the angels. The question was which side were the angels on? Mark went down the steps in a puzzled frame of mind. His inquiries so far were just taking him round in circles. If he, Sellingby and Harrap, the police and Geoff Randall were all on the same side, who was against them? Mrs Breedon was dead and Lou . . . ? About Lou he did not know nor at the moment did he want to. All he wanted to know was where she was. Was she safe? There would be time to examine her part in it when he had found her. She was his wife. He could not afford to allow himself the luxury of suspicions. That only left him with one more point of contact. He turned up his coat collar and went in search of Edward Kelsey.

★　★　★

The rhododendrons dripped incessantly. Mark stood and watched a silver drop glide down the centre groove of a dark leaf and fall like a tear from the point, suspended for a moment in mid-air before disintegrating to splash on the surface of the leaf below. A slight haze caused by condensation had formed on the glass so he seemed to be looking through the soft focus of a camera lens. The effect of mist and falling light was mesmerising.

Mr. Kelsey came in with two coffee cups balanced on a wicker tray which he set down on a low table in the centre of the room.

'I'm sorry, Mark,' he said, causing his visitor to turn round, 'but this time I really can't help you. I don't know where Lou is.'

'You knew last time?'

Kelsey handed him a cup and sat down looking a trifle guilty. 'Yes,' he admitted. 'Lou came to see me in a very distressed state. She was convinced someone was trying to kill her. I arranged for Mrs. Breedon to hide her until we could find out what was going on.'

'Mrs. Breedon's dead. Did you know?'

'I heard. Shocking. The way violence has become a part of our everyday experience is appalling.'

'Blame it on T.V.' said Mark flatly.

'It has something to do with it, I think,' commented Mr. Kelsey thoughtfully. 'You can hardly submit people to a barrage of realistic violent images and then expect them still to be able to draw the fine line between the make-believe and the real. It numbs the senses and as the old saying has it, where there's no sense there's no feeling.'

'Lou wasn't there.'

'You checked?'

'There was only one body. I saw them carrying in the stretcher. I went in after the ambulance left. There was no one there.'

'Perhaps she escaped.'

'Perhaps they took her.'

'Hooligans. Kids they said. Why would they?'

Mark shrugged. 'I don't know.'

'Perhaps she heard them, saw what had happened, got scared and ran away,' pointed out Mr. Kelsey comfortingly.

'Perhaps.'

There was a short silence as both men drank their coffee. The alternative was something neither of them cared to contemplate.

Mark spoke to dispel the thought.

'What made you change your mind?'

'About what?'

'About me. I take it you had me down as chief suspect. What made you decide to let me know where Lou was?'

Mr. Kelsey smiled. 'That was Mrs. Breedon. Very sentimental woman. Romantic to the core. You were so obviously distressed by

Lou's disappearance she felt sure your affection for her was genuine. She — that is we thought it would be cruel to make you suffer any longer. We decided to trust you.'

'And now?'

Mr. Kelsey waved self-deprecatingly. 'It appears someone doesn't trust me.'

'What makes you say that?'

'If Lou is on the run she hasn't come to me, that's all I can tell you.'

The telephone rang. It was a small set with a quiet purr. Mark couldn't tell at first where it was coming from but Mr. Kelsey went to retrieve it from a small corner table hidden by one of the armchairs.

'Yes?' he said, then after a moment. 'Everything all right?' A pause, then 'You can tell him yourself. He's here. Just a moment.'

He held the receiver out to Mark. 'It's your wife.'

Mark leaped up nearly spilling the contents of his coffee cup all over him. Mr. Kelsey deftly removed it from his hands thus saving the carpet. In the same instant Mark grabbed the receiver.

'Lou? Lou darling?'

'Hello, Mark.' She sounded far away. The line crackled badly.

'Are you all right?'

'Yes, I'm fine,' she said. 'Don't worry.'

'Where are you?'

She hesitated. 'I can't say.'

'Why can't you?'

'I just can't. Not at the moment. I just wanted to let you know I'm all right. You needn't worry.'

'Of course I'm worried. Where the hell are you?'

'I really can't say, Mark.' She was pleading with him. Her voice trembled, or was it just the effect of the poor line? 'Please . . . I love you.'

'I love you, too, darling.' It sounded pathetic. 'Everthing's going to be fine.'

'Yes.' She sounded a little brighter as if she found comfort in his reassurance, although God knows it was made without foundation.

'Must go now,' she said quickly.

'Wait a minute . . . '

'Must go,' she repeated. '*Tempus fugit*

and all that, Mark. Remember?'

'Lou . . . ?' he began but she had rung off. The dialling tone burred loudly in his ear. He replaced the receiver.

'She says she's all right,' said Edward Kelsey encouragingly.

'Yes.' Mark felt dazed. Their conversation had been so short he had hardly taken any of it in.

'She didn't say where?' asked Kelsey anxiously.

Mark shook his head. 'She wouldn't say. They must have her.'

He sank into the armchair and propped his chin up with one hand in the very image of 'The Thinker'. It was a suitable pose. He was racking his brains.

'Mark?' inquired Mr. Kelsey tentatively, as if he hardly dared asked. 'Who are *they*?'

Mark looked up for a moment, his concentration broken. 'That's the trouble,' he said desperately. 'I haven't a bloody clue.'

# 18

The London train was on time. It came hurtling through the darkness appearing like a spectre in the customary mists that gathered in the valley at this time of evening in the twilight end of the year. Ravenhill was a misty town.

Mark waited at the end of the platform for the passengers to disembark. He spotted Rufford at once, as soon as he was disgorged from the carriage. He could hardly be inconspicuous given his size. As soon as he saw Mark he gave a cheery wave.

'Whitherto?' he inquired as he passed through the ticket barrier.

'The Castle Hotel is across the road,' Mark told him. 'That's generally fairly quiet about this time. We can talk there.'

'Fine.'

The two men walked in silence across the station forecourt. Conversation was in any case virtually impossible with the noise of buses and taxis revving their engines waiting to pick up and put down, and clang of trolleys and the continuous shunt of engines in the goods sidings that bordered the road. The mist seemed thicker outside the station possibly because the lights were less bright. It was a cold damp shroud. A little Christmas tree decked with coloured fairy lights reminded them of forthcoming cheer but for the moment there didn't seem much of it around.

The Castle Hotel stood on the far side of the cobbled forecourt, which was in the form of a large triangle. The station, an old Victorian model which unsuccessfully tried to combine old and new with a section of modern frontage, occupied one side and the hotel, flanked by a few olde worlde shops, the other. The third side was taken up by the main road leading into the town centre. Beyond that was a very high brick wall marking the perimeter of a small industrial estate. Neither Mark nor Rufford found this of any interest. They turned their attention to the hotel.

Which castle it was named after was a mystery because there were none in Ravenhill, except an ancient Iron Age fort the foundations of which were now securely preserved under Woolworth's. The picture on the signboard romantically portrayed a crumbling ruin overlooking the sea, which was, at its nearest point, a good hundred miles away. The building itself bore no outward traces of an aristocratic past. It was a large square house with white-washed walls and black paintwork. A pair of wrought-iron tubs, which in summer were filled with flowers, squatted either side of the entrance. The door was open and a mellow amber light glowed from within.

Mark led the way into the lounge bar.

The interior of the Castle was a pleasant surprise, since its exterior was neat but not prepossessing. A narrow corridor led first to the bar, which occupied one side of the hall. This was meticulously kept. Spotless glasses gleamed on their racks like a regiment on parade, the copper bar-top shone and sparkled in the subdued lighting. The old-fashioned ceramic hand-pumps were polished until they reflected the glow like mirrors. The walls of the hall were panelled and a spiral wooden staircaise led up in one corner to a restaurant on the first floor. Opposite the bar forming an L-shaped room, was the lounge, reached through an archway so low Rufford and Mark had to bend to avoid the beam. Once in the room Rufford gave a deep sigh of satisfaction.

The lounge was not furnished like a bar at all but more like the sitting room of a slightly impoverished country house. It was a small, cosy room panelled from floor to ceiling like the hallway. The wall lights were old-fashioned brass sconces, covered by tiny red tasselled shades that gave out a warm light. A real log fire crackled in the grate of what appeared to be a quite genuine Adam fireplace. The house, unlike many a modern public house, was a true antique and the furniture very nearly matched its style. Instead of the usual plastic or nylon velvet covered seats the lounge was supplied with large armchairs, winged and comfortable, upholstered in tapestry and figured brocades, albeit a little threadbare and faded. Rufford sank into the largest and leaned back closing his eyes.

'Now this,' he said blissfully, 'is what I call a pub. Home from home.'

Mark grinned and went to buy a round of drinks at the bar. When he came back he pulled up a chair opposite so they could talk privately.

'What have you got to tell me?' he asked, as soon as Rufford had had a chance to taste his beer.

Rufford smacked his lips and set his glass down. 'I've found out who Geoff's contact at the MOD was — wait for it — none other than our old friend Marcus Sellingby.'

'Sellingby?'

'Coincidence what?'

'I'll say. It was Sellingby then who warned Geoff against contacting me?'

'So it appears. Sellingby was quite happy to use your wife but he didn't want you involved.'

'Did you find out why not?'

'You tell me.'

'I might steal his thunder perhaps. Is he after promotion?'

'Who isn't? He's certainly keeping things to himself. No one at the MOD knows anything about it.'

'Unusual.'

'Very. They usually need at least three signatures to go to the toilet. If Sellingby *is* straight he's running a maverick operation.'

'What about our man from EDS?'

'Ditto.'

'*Harrap?*' said Mark incredulously.

'Is supposed to be on his way to Korea to tell our oriental friends which way their rockets should be pointing.'

'Who's behind it? K.G.B.?'

Rufford shook his head. 'Not according to our intelligence boys. Looks more like a bit of private enterprise they think, involving an African based company. Ostensibly a legitimate broker's in Salisbury. Small arms dealer. Shotguns, air rifles — strictly for farmers. A lot of people would be interested in a deal like this, not all of them on the other side. Panavia, Lufthansa and all their little subsidiaries wouldn't half like a piece of the action.'

'This company in Salisbury. Data processing provided by INSOFT — right?'

'*Mais naturellement.* Simple computer interface with Head Office. International carrier link direct to INSOFT databank England. Accounts, invoicing, personnel records the lot. Sent weekly. Hello, hello . . . ?'

Rufford trailed off suddenly as his attention was caught by a man standing at the bar. The man was half-turned away from him waiting for the barman to serve him, but Rufford caught a glimpse of a dark, swarthy face that he recognised. The man was in his forties but wore his hair quite long and in a style reminiscent of the early sixties. His drooping Mexican-style moustache also dated him. He wore a dark city suit and looked like a conventional businessman. Only the length of his hair and a liberal display of flashy gold jewellery suggested his line of business was out of the ordinary. He downed his drink quickly, exchanged a few words with the barman and went upstairs to the restaurant without seeing the two men in the lounge, who were partly obscured from his view by the pillar of the archway and the deep wings of their armchairs.

'Who is he?' inquired Mark softly, seeing Rufford was fairly riveted by the sight of him.

'Piet de Wint,' explained Rufford. 'Played wingthreequarter for the Springboks in the winter of 'Fifty-nine to Sixty, I think it was.'

'Really?' Mark was not a sportsman. His indifference showed.

Rufford cast him an impatient glance. 'Mercenary.'

'I thought all sportsmen were nowadays.'

'No, fathead. That's his profession. Soldier of fortune to put it politely.'

'*That* sort of mercenary.'

'The last I heard of him,' Rufford mused quietly half to himself, 'he was languishing in an East African jail preparatory to getting the chop.'

'Evidently he didn't get it.'

'Evidently. I wonder what brings him to Ravenhill.'

'Possibly he's looking for somewhere to live a quiet life,' offered Mark blandly.

'I doubt it. This begins to look nasty, old thing.'

'Begins?'

Rufford looked stern. 'I don't want you tangling with the likes of Piet de Wint. With due respect to your manhood he is the likes of which you cannot handle. Don't forget I'm — '

'Short-staffed,' Mark chimed in dutifully. 'Don't worry. I'm not about to go fifteen rounds with an ex-Aardvark.'

Rufford threw him a withering look. 'Springbok.'

'Sorry.'

'I think you'd better leave him to me. You didn't join this enterprise to be a bloody hero. You're just supposed to be the clever clogs.'

'What are you going to do?' asked Mark suspiciously.

Rufford's eyes widened angelically. 'There are times,' he observed practically, 'when it is prudent to take a man out of the game.'

'Nothing unsporting, Ian, surely?'

Rufford raised his eyebrows in faint hauteur. He knew when he was being mocked. 'There is such a thing as a fair tackle.'

Mark laughed. 'Nowadays they call it a professional foul.'

Rufford's look withered him a bit more. 'Rugby Union,' he pointed out loftily, 'is an *amateur* game.'

Mark bowed to his superior knowledge. 'All right. I'll leave him to you.'

'Do that,' ordered the team captain. 'Just you concentrate on finding the tapes.'

'And Lou.'

'Looks as if that's one and the same thing, doesn't it?'

Mark lowered his gaze as if reluctant to meet an accusation.

'Yes,' he admitted, then raising his voice a little he went on, 'So far, all we know, as I see it, is that Sellingby was Geoff Randall's contact, Harrap isn't where he ought to be, there's a tame

221

gorilla running round the streets of Ravenhill and my wife's disappeared.'

'Exactly. Confusing, isn't it?' Rufford's smile was benevolent. 'I trust you'll have it all sorted out by the end of the week. I've got another job for you.'

Mark snorted derisively. 'What now?' he spread his hands to indicate his helplessness. Rufford put the empty glasses into them. 'Same again.'

Mark looked down at them and grimaced. 'Is this on expenses?' Rufford looked shocked. 'Oh, no, dear boy. You're paying.'

★ ★ ★

Through the mist in the dark streets the golden headlights of the car shone steadily. The car was stationary. Three men sat in it heavily muffled in thick dark overcoats. Another car, a white, unmarked saloon, hugged the kerb at the other end of the street. Apart from these two the road was deserted. The dark buildings on either side were factories, at this time of night unlit except for the odd lamp burning over an entrance. The street lights were so weak as to make little impression on the mist and shadows.

One of the men got out of the car and lit a cigarette, cupping it in his hands to encourage the glow to warm the ends of his fingers. It was a very cold night, likely to freeze before morning.

The man walked up and down a few times then leaned against the car waiting.

A few moments later he heard a man approaching and looking up he tossed the cigarette aside, stuck his hands in his pockets and went to meet him.

They came within range of each other under a street lamp in the ochre haze of which they could see each other's faces.

'Piet de Wint?' inquired Sergeant Knutter pleasantly.

The dark South African halted and eyed him cautiously. Knutter's pale blue eyes twinkled back at him through the gilded curtain of light that divided them.

'Yes?' he replied with a note of surprise in his voice. 'Who are you?'

Sergeant Knutter smiled sociably. 'I'm a police officer, sir.' He withdrew one hand from his coat pocket to show his warrant card. 'I'm afraid I must ask you to come along with me.'

De Wint gave a short, embarrassed laugh. 'What for?'

Sergeant Knutter had turned away as if expecting him to follow. He turned back. 'I'm arresting you, sir.'

'What for?' repeated the South African, slightly more belligerently this time.

'Oh numerous crimes sir,' explained Knutter airly. 'Let's see now. Smuggling arms on to her Majesty's sovereign soil. Possessing same without a licence. Robbery with violence. There's that small matter of causing a breach of the peace in a certain East African territory with which Her Majesty's Britannic Government has an extradition treaty — sorry about that . . . and lately but not least the murder of one Geoffrey Stephen Randall. Also your car is not taxed.'

'It's a hire car.'

Knutter was all sympathy. 'Even so, sir.'

★　★　★

He nodded over de Wint's shoulder to the two burly figures who had silently positioned themselves behind him to cut off any retreat. The other two men in the car nearest them also got out and stationed themselves to block a sudden sprint across the road. De Wint was a professional. He noted they were all armed.

'These gentlemen will give you a lift,' offered Knutter helpfully. 'It's not far to the station but we don't expect our guests to walk.'

De Wint shrugged. He knew when to give himself up. He allowed himself to be directed to the white car and helped into the back seat.

'I shall want to call my solicitor,' he observed curtly.

Sergeant Knutter nodded. 'That wouldn't be Mr. Hetherington, would it?' he inquired, 'Of Hetherington, Hertford and Mortison?'

De Wint shot him a dirty look. 'Why?'

'I'm afraid he's just been detained. Corruption of a jury, I believe. Nasty business. However we do keep a list of local solicitors in the station. All qualified. You could try one of them.'

De Wint scowled. Knutter closed the door on him and climbed into his own car.

The headlights of the two cars formed a lake of amber in the centre of the road, then they swung round to form a cavalcade and glided away.

★ ★ ★

When Mark got home he was dead-beat. He flung himself into the rocking chair in the kitchen and pulled the old tartan rug over him. A can of lager stood on the cupboard. He reached up for this and yanked the ring off to open it. To reach a glass he would have to get up. He kicked off his shoes and settled for a mug out of the cupboard instead.

He lay back gently rocking himself to induce a feeling of relaxation watching the long second-hand tick round on the face of the old mantel-clock that stood on the dresser. It had a very loud tick. It was nearly midnight. On the hour it would chime softly, a mellow mellifluous tone that Mark had grown to like. The clock in its polished walnut case was so old its ivory face had darkened to yellow and the inscription on the brass plate affixed just below the dial was barely legible. *Tempus fugit* it said in neat engraved italics. Indeed it did, Mark thought vaguely. His mind refused to concentrate properly on this idea or any other he was so weary. He tried to focus it. Time was flying and he had reached no conclusions.

Faces swam across his consciousness. The news about Sellingby changed the scenario. He envisaged his smooth oval face and cold marble eyes. Harrap was a shifty, nervous little character — out of his depth perhaps. Lou was beautiful. He would think nothing ill of her — not yet. Who else? Mrs. Breedon . . . Something suddenly clicked in his brain reference Mrs. Breedon. She was not dead. He sat up suddenly, stirred by the certainty of his conviction. Intuition is the name given to the workings of the sub-conscious. The facts had been lying there dormant all along. She was a sentimental woman

Edward Kelsey had said. There had been only one thing missing that he could see — the portrait of Rosa Luxemburg. Not the kind of thing a thief would take, it was the kind of thing a sentimental woman who had cherished it for years could not leave behind.

Mark frowned. He had seen the ambulance and the police car with his own eyes. Someone had gone to a great deal of trouble to stage-manage a death. For somebody to arrange that kind of official 'disappearance' they would need a lot of clout, for both police car and ambulance were genuine, he was sure of that.

Mark sank back in the chair and closed his eyes. The moving finger having writ moved on and in the mists of his imagination it seemed to be definitely pointing in one direction. The trouble was he was so damn tired he could hardly focus on the person it was pointing out to him. The name was just forming in letters of fire in his brain when he fell fast asleep.

# 19

Mark woke. A heavy silence hung over the kitchen like a pall. He tried to shake the sleep from his head and squeezed his eyes to focus them again. He was still in the armchair wrapped in an old tartan rug. As he stirred he kicked an empty lager tin which rolled noisily across the tiled floor, breaking the uncanny silence. It came to rest at the foot of the dresser and silence ruled once more.

Mark didn't like it. It was too quiet. Unnaturally quiet. Something was wrong. He got unsteadily to his feet and stared at the old clock. It was half-past mid-night. He frowned and looked out of the window. Dawn was already beginning to break over the curve of the hill. A pink sheen was slowly spreading across a pearly sky. It must be gone eight.

He picked up the clock. It was a big, heavy timepiece. Carefully Mark scruti-nised it, then the truth forced itself into his sleep-heavy brain. It had stopped. That was the explanation for the disturbing silence in the kitchen. He had grown accustomed to the steady tick-tock.

He replaced the clock and filled the kettle, which he placed on the stove, then, while he waited for it to boil, he picked up the clock again and took it back to his chair.

He prised the glass front open and adjusted the ornate hands to match the time flashed up on his digital watch. He ran a finger over the smooth worn engraving that decorated the face. It was a very fine old clock.

He pushed the glass back into position and turned the clock over to wind it. As he did so a gleam of new metal caught his eye. The brass plate covering the works had been tampered with. A clean score had been made by a sharp knife or a screwdriver. Someone had recently been trying to open the clock.

Intrigued, Mark reached for a kitchen knife and prised off the plate. It came away quite easily. Inside he found two coils of computer tape.

He took them out then replaced the back, wound the clock and set it on the dresser where it went on marking time with its usual regularity. The kettle whistled. He poured himself a cup of coffee, then sat and contemplated his discovery.

Lou had tried to tell him. He realised that now. Her parting words were '*Tempus Fugit*', an expression she never normally used. He should have guessed. He looked at the face of the old clock, gradually browning at the edges like a piece of underdone toast, with its worn engraving and laughed out loud. It was so simple he would never have thought of it, then another thought crossed his mind and he was serious again. Lou had trusted him to find the tapes but she couldn't tell him where she was. What did that mean?

He picked up the tapes and wrapped them in cling film to protect the surface. All he needed now was a large computer sophisticated enough to read them and confirm that they were indeed what he was looking for. Fortunately he knew just where to find one.

The low, rolling hills of Leicestershire are bare and bleak in the winter. Cold east winds sweep across them. The valleys are too shallow for shelter and there are few trees. The magnificent summer corn-fields are ploughed and fallow. There are few signs of habitation between the remote, scattered villages. In Leicestershire you wonder what people mean when they say these islands are over-crowded.

Mark directed his car down the old Roman road which ran like a straight white spine along the ridges, always sticking to the high ground. Mark wondered idly why those wily ancestors had chosen such an elevated route. Possible solutions flickered through his brain — drainage, safety from ambush, in Roman times the saucer-like valleys must have been thickly forested, a bloody-minded determination to take the direct route no matter what. His car ran smoothly over the tarmac. He could see his way for miles. There was not another vehicle on the road. Away in the blue distance he could see his destination.

To the left a long way ahead of him yet lay a long arching hill like an upturned saucer crowned with trees. It stood out as one of the few thickly wooded slopes in the district, a small reminder of the ancient forests that had been cleared to make way for the expanding farms and buried to form coalfields. The trees were bare and their black outlines bristled against the grey sky, which was darkening by the minute for it was by now late afternoon.

Mark drove on until he came under the shadow of the long hill, then turned left into a narrow lane. A black and white signpost placed at the junction pointed the way to *Minstead Parva*. A church steeple poking up through the trees at the foot of the hill proclaimed the whereabouts of the village but Mark wasn't going so far. He turned off again into a climbing, meandering access road following a hand-painted sign to 'The Laurels'.

'The Laurels' had once been a gracious country mansion built at the turn of the century in imitation-Jacobean style in an elevated position with unparalleled views across the vale of Minstead, taking in the two parishes, Parva and Magna, and the open, uninterrupted countryside beyond. The tall twisted chimneys and upper casements of the house were just visible through the trees, although in summer when the trees were in leaf and the banks of rhododendrons that surrounded it were in bloom, its privacy was absolute. Although the view from the house was magnificent, from the road it was all but invisible. It was further protected by a ten-foot high perimeter fence.

Mark parked his car in a rough passing-place in the lane and walked up to the gatehouse. The security guard was reading a newspaper. Mark flashed a credit card and a smile at him simultaneously. The guard nodded and smiled in return. Mark walked through on to the site.

EDS (Midland) Ltd — Research Laboratories developed in a haphazard way. Founded during the Second World War to provide facilities for the development of the then recently discovered radar the site originally consisted of

Nissen huts and long, single storey brick buildings clustered around the old, dignified house which had been taken over by the old War Department. As the pace of electronic warfare increased beyond all expectations and the budgets beyond the scope of ordinary government departments the house had been taken over by private enterprise and the Nissen huts gave way to Portakabins, which were assembled in a 'village' on the front lawn. The occasional small radio mast or dish receiver gave a clue to the interests of the work-force but no newcomer would have guessed from their poor appearance that EDS (Midland) Ltd. — Research Laboratories were the home of the latest developments in homing and guidance for sophisticated weaponry, radar systems for both military and domestic use and the advanced technology involved in satellite communications. In Britain scientists are still expected to work in potting sheds. Visiting Americans stared in disbelief at Britain's contribution to the space race. To the naked eye it resembled an internment camp.

Some efforts nevertheless were being made to modernise. The lower section of the site which stretched some way down the hill, was a building site. A faceless modern block of concrete was being constructed with few windows and no character to house the Satellite Communications Division. A second, discreetly sunk into a shallow depression, was already in use. Mark made for this building. This was the home of the E.W. Division — Electronic Warfare.

Before he reached it he paused and bent to tie his laces, at the same time keeping his eye on the entrance. The building, known as 'Barnes Wallis House' after the inventor, was a 'secure' building. It could only be entered by someone using a card key — a piece of plastic about the size of a credit card bearing a staff number which could be read by a computer controlling entry of personnel. Mark, however, knew that there is one area in which humans have the edge over computers. They are entirely unpredictable.

He watched a pretty young secretary

laden with documents trip past him. A card key was attached to her belt by a long chain. His strategy was simplicity itself. He straightened up and followed close behind her.

She made for the side door and inserted the key into the slot beside the upright. While she struggled to shift the weight of her burden so that she could open the door and remove the key at the same time, Mark swiftly moved up behind her and held the door open for her. She smiled gratefully. He smiled in return and followed her into the building. There are times when chivalry is worth more than a whole course in karate.

Just inside the door stood a full-size (about fifteen feet long), dark-green model of the new XL-597 missile the 'Cloudskimmer' which someone had facetiously hung a label on christening it the 'Windbreaker'. A cup of coffee and half a sandwich reposed forlornly on the tailfin. Above it, in a series of colour photographs, Tornado and Harrier aircraft soared into the wide, blue yonder.

The 'Cloudskimmer' was displayed in

a small entrance hall at the end of which were double doors marked 'SKYRANGER MARK III LAB — NO ADMITTANCE TO UNAUTHO-RISED PERSONNEL'. Through the windows there were signs of activity as young men in faded jeans and check shirts strolled between banks of electronic equipment. It was not quite the scene imagined in many a James Bond epic. There were no white coats here and no tidy consoles. Wires had a great tendency to hang out of everything, including the pockets of the young men patrolling the lab. Some of the equipment was old, some new, some evidently improvised and none of it seemed to make a matching set. A computer terminal sat at the end of one of the benches with a sign on it prohibiting the playing of Space Invaders. A blackboard was covered with scrawled formulae in illegible handwriting. Not much scope for a spy in what was evidently a hotbed of illiteracy.

Mark gave the scene only a cursory

glance. He knew from a past visit as an 'INSOFT' designer working under contract to EDS that the computer room was in a well-protected bunker. To reach it he had to go down. A side door revealed a narrow stairwell. Down this he went.

At the bottom of the stairs a white anonymous corridor led into another white anonymous corridor. This in turn led him to a heavy steel door. Beside it a notice commanded that '*NO FOOD OR DRINK SHALL BE TAKEN INTO THE COMPUTER ROOM*'. Below the notice another slot was set into the wall to accept a card key supplied only to authorised members of staff. Along the wall in the corridor were a series of vending machines dispensing hot drinks for computer-room staff and a chair was thoughtfully provided for them so they could take their elevenses without being tempted to break the written rule. Mark dug in his pocket for the necessary change and helped himself to a cup of coffee. He sat on the chair and waited.

He had finished his coffee and was staring into the bottom of the cup when a golden-haired girl came along the corridor towards him. He smiled at her and she smiled pleasantly in return. She took out her card key and slotted it into the wall. Mark leaped up and chivalrously held the door open for her. She thanked him politely and they both stepped through. He had for the second time that day reason to thank his mother for bringing him up to be well-mannered towards young ladies.

The steel door did not lead directly into the computer room but into a small antechamber where another steel door awaited them. Mark closed the outer door behind him. The inner door was opened by means of a steam lock. The girl pressed the red button to operate it and they heard the hiss as the steam escaped. Mark smiled apologetically for standing so close to the girl, which he could hardly help doing there being so little space. The girl grinned cheerfully in acknowledgement. 'Bit of a squash,' she remarked gamely, evidently not minding the inconvenience. When all the steam had been released she pushed the door open to allow them both to enter the computer room.

The underground chamber had no windows. It was divided into two sections by a glass partition. Through the glass Mark could see the main computer — a row of metal cabinets the top half of which were covered by transparent windows so that it was possible to see the huge tape wheels turning inside. The half of the room he was standing in was furnished with low benches along which computer terminals were aligned at regular intervals. Their flickering screens gave off a white light that imparted a slightly eerie atmosphere to the otherwise softly lit area. The room was very quiet except for the occasional ticker-tacker of the terminal keyboards which were almost noiseless. All the operators worked in silence and deep concentration, their eyes on the screen in front of them. It was very cold. Mark shivered as soon as he walked in. The room was air-conditioned to keep the machines at the right temperature, which was chosen for their comfort and not that of their human operators. It was not quite a 'cave of ice' but it was very nearly.

In front of him stood a low cabinet on top of which lay an open folder. A notice in large letters exhorted him to sign in and out as company regulations demanded. He scrawled an illegible signature in the appropriate column and in the space marked 'Project Number' jotted a friend's five figure telephone number. He took the tapes out of his pocket and strolled across the technician whose little office bridged the two halves of the chamber.

'A friend of mine from Cincinnati Electronics has sent me some information I asked for,' he said drily holding up the tapes, 'and look how he's sent it. What's wrong with a letter I ask? Can you run these so I can see what he's got to say for himself?'

The technician grinned. 'Sure. He might have made it a cassette. It would have been easier.'

Mark grimaced. 'He was always a bit of a showoff.' The technician nodded to a

vacant seat at one of the benches.
'Terminal Seven is free.'

He disappeared into the prohibited
section to wind the tapes on to spools and
fit them into the computer. Mark
sauntered across to Terminal Seven and
waited for him to give him the thumbs-up
sign.

A white light jigged in the corner of the
screen. The technician gave him the nod
to tell him he was on-line. Mark began to
type in the call-up code.

(INSOFTDATA.)

The light danced across the screen and
came back with

WHO ARE YOU?

Please, corrected Mark mentally, then
typed in MCNAMARA.

The light hesitated, then flashed across
and back and printed brusquely

EH? INPUT INCORRECT. PLEASE
RE-INPUT.

Mark received this information phleg-
matically and responded with

LOUISE MCNAMARA.

The light pranced across the screen
again and repeated its message

EH? INPUT INCORRECT. PLEASE RE-INPUT.

Mark frowned. Surely Lou had used her own name? He floundered for a moment then inspiration came to his rescue. He keyed in

LOUISE VERONICA MCNAMARA.

The light flashed across the screen and came back with

PASSWORD?

Mark felt a small glow of satisfaction. So far so good. Not many people knew about the Veronica. It was a name Lou hated. She never used it but it was on the marriage certificate. Now came the difficult bit. When in doubt, he reasoned, try the obvious. He typed in the program title

XANADU

The screen flashed up its favourite legend.

EH? INPUT INCORRECT. PLEASE RE-INPUT.

Damn, thought Mark. He had come so far. What would Louise have used for a password? She was his wife. He ought to be able to second guess her. He knew how her mind worked, at least he thought he did. The trouble was she didn't think like he did. There were times when she didn't think logically at all. She had a woman's butterfly mind, intuitive, lateral in its direction. She worked by association of ideas as often as not. Mark closed his eyes for a moment and tried by sheer strength of will to force some kind of telepathic link with his wife. As he concentrated a mental image of the kitchen clock seemed to occupy his thoughts. He opened his eyes and stared at the blank screen. It didn't seem to have much to do with what he was dealing with but he had no other ideas so he keyed in the magic words

TEMPUS FUGIT.

The light hesitated. 'Go on,' he urged silently. It *was* magic. The light danced across the screen and came back with the words he was waiting to see

WELCOME TO THE XANADU PROGRAM.

Mark nearly whooped with triumph. He keyed in the command

PLATFORM ONE

and let the program run.

He sat for some time watching an endless procession of facts and figures pass before his eyes, arrays, elevations, graphics and statistics, Occasionally he jotted something down to give the impression he was absorbing what he saw. In fact it meant nothing to him. All he knew was he had struck gold. These were the precious tapes. He had bargaining power.

After a decent interval he logged out and went to ask the technician to return the tapes, which were duly handed over and stuffed in his pocket. He signed out and left the computer room already feeling the cold. He smiled and nodded to one or two people he passed on his way out of the building and left the security guard with a jovial remark about England's prospects of retaining the Ashes on their forthcoming Australian tour which had him falling off his chair. His mother always said his happy knack of getting on with people would take him anywhere. Mark looked back at the high wire fence and grinned at the thought. If only she knew.

He found his car where he had left it, reversed it down the lane and set off back the way he had come.

It was already quite dark and beginning to rain heavily. He turned his headlights full on turning the wet lane into the golden river of which he felt himself to be the proverbial king. He turned on the radio. A horn concerto by Mozart filled the car with soothing, civilised sounds. He pom-pommed along with it until he spotted a phone box, then he swerved into the side of the road and stopped.

Rufford was in the office when he rang.

'I've got the tapes,' was his introduction.

'Good man.' Rufford sounded surprised.

'They've got Lou, Ian.'

There was a slight pause. 'Are you sure?'

'Positive. I think I've got it worked out.'

'Good man,' Rufford echoed himself. He sounded distant. The rain was beating against the phone box making a terrific noise.

'I can't give them back. Not yet. I've

got to use them to get Lou back. I've got to arrange a trade.'

Rufford didn't answer.

'You do understand,' Mark was almost pleading with him, 'I've got to put my wife first, country or no bloody country. Without the tapes she's got no chance.'

Rufford's voice came back soothingly, although slightly strained by the poor quality of the line. 'All right, Mark. We're not the SAS. Do what you think best. You're in charge. If anyone asks you haven't phoned me.'

'Thanks, friend.'

A thin chuckle escaped down the line. 'We've kept our side of the contract. We only said we'd locate the tapes. We never said anything about giving them back.'

'Are you sure?'

'I always read the small print. Strains your eyes but saves a lot of indigestion.'

'She is my wife. I owe her.' Mark said by way of an explanation.

Rufford was sympathetic. 'Of course. Family before friends, friends before country. But Mark — ' he stopped short.

'What?'

'Be bloody careful, old son.'

Mark laughed. 'I know. You're short-staffed.' 'Just be bloody careful, that's all,' Rufford said sternly and hung up.

Mark climbed back into his car. The horn concerto had given way to an operatic tenor. He couldn't sing along with that so he switched it off. The car wheels screeched as he accelerated quickly out on to the wet road. He knew he had the ace of trumps. All he had to do now was pick the right moment to play it.

# 20

Sergeant Knutter walked up the hill with his hands stuck in his pockets, whistling a tuneless and unrecognisable air. His wispy hair blew upwards as if he had had a fright and the end of his nose was red-tipped with cold.

The sky was a fine pastel blue streaked with mares' tails skittering across the hills. It was a pleasant morning, fresh and bright but the wind had a bitter edge to it.

When he reached the McNamaras' cottage he thumped on the door and waited. Mark's car was parked outside so he was confident of finding him in.

Mark opened the door only half-dressed. He had obviously just got up. He was yawning and running a hand through his tousled ginger curls. Knutter looked at his watch. It was gone ten.

'Good morning, sir,' he began politely. 'Sorry to disturb you.'

Mark allowed him to enter. 'That's all right.' he said ruefully. 'I overslept, I'm afraid. I had rather a sleepless night. I must have dropped off just as it was time to get up.'

He ran a hand down his front and realised he had nothing on above the waist. He grabbed a shirt from a pile of unironed washing that sat on the splintered table and began struggling into it.

Sergeant Knutter fished in his pocket. 'I've got a warrant here somewhere.'

Mark paused half-in, half-out of his shirt and looked up sharply. 'Warrant?'

Knutter smiled benignly. 'Search warrant. We have reason to believe your wife may have hidden certain 'evidence' on these premises. It may help us to find out what's become of her.'

Mark shrugged his shirt on. 'Oh, I see,' he said lamely. 'Well, go ahead.'

'Thank you, sir. Very co-operative of you.'

Mark left him methodically searching through the dresser in the living room, turning out one drawer at a time and neatly replacing the contents when he had sorted through them. He had obviously done this sort of thing many times before. Mark made them both a cup of coffee and returned to the living room.

'Don't forget the clock,' he said cheerfully, handing one of the cups over.

'Clock?' Sergeant Knutter looked bemused.

'In the kitchen,' Mark explained. 'On the kitchen dresser. Don't people usually hide things in clocks?'

Sergeant Knutter chuckled richly. 'Only in films I think, but I'll bear it in mind.'

'Just a suggestion.' Mark watched him curiously for a moment. 'What exactly is it you're looking for?'

The sergeant hesitated for a second then said evenly, 'A tape, sir, or tapes. Computer tape.'

'Wouldn't that be on a cassette?' inquired Mark knowledgeably.

Knutter shook his head. 'No, sir. It would be for a large computer. Tape about an inch wide maybe. Like a big roll of Sellotape.'

'There's a Sellotape tin in the bottom

drawer,' offered Mark helpfully.

Knutter pulled open the bottom drawer. The tin was lying in full view. He took it out and inspected it.

'It *is* Sellotape,' he declared. 'You wouldn't have come across these tapes by any chance?'

'No.'

'You wouldn't want to make off with them at all?'

'Wouldn't need to.'

Knutter sat back on his haunches and examined Mark speculatively. 'Now what do you mean by that?' he admonished severely.

Mark returned his direct gaze unflinchingly. He was not at all put out by the straight question. He laughed and made himself comfortable in the easy chair.

'Let me explain something to you,' he said generously. 'Whoever stole these tapes you're looking for — I take it they are stolen?' Knutter refrained from comment so Mark carried on. 'They contain confidential information anyway. Right?'

Knutter nodded. 'So we're given to understand.'

'Whoever took them in the first place,' Mark told him frankly, 'is an amateur.'

'How do you make that out?'

Mark made a sweeping gesture with his hand. 'No need.'

Knutter was genuinely interested. 'They'd need to get the tapes to get the information surely?'

Mark shook his head. 'Not these days. Spying by computer is a different game to the old cloak-and-dagger business. No leg-work. No hanging about on dark corners waiting for microfilm to be dropped in the litter bin. It's all a matter of mathematics.'

'Come again?'

'All you need to penetrate is a very sophisticated mathematical formula. It's like safe-breaking. Once you've worked out the combination you can crack the whole computer network.'

Knutter let out a long hissing sigh. 'Is that a fact?'

Mark nodded and leaned forward to impart confidentially, 'The beauty of it is no one knows you've penetrated until the other side, whoever they are, start using your secrets. Until then you've no way of knowing they've been stolen and they can be on the other side of the world when the theft occurs.'

★ ★ ★

Knutter's jaw dropped open. 'That's not possible surely?'

Mark pointed to the ceiling. ' "There are more things in heaven and earth, Horatio, than are dreamt of in your philosophy'. Satellite communications make on-line computing possible on a global scale. It's not like the old days when an agent had to spend years trying to work himself into a position of trust so that he could get his hand in the filing cabinet. All you need now is a Phd in Pure Mathematics, a course in software design and a telephone.'

★ ★ ★

Knutter looked amazed. 'You're joking. It's not possible.'

'The Russians are already at it. The best mathematicians can work out how to penetrate a computer up to Cray-I level and they don't even have to leave Vladivostok.'

'What's Cray-I?'

'American-built machines for top-security use. Repositories of classified information. The government uses machines of that type to store military secrets.'

Knutter's eyes widened innocently. 'How the hell do you know?'

Mark grinned impishly and his eyes danced. 'I read the papers I work for. It's a matter of real concern in financial circles. Not only government departments are vulnerable. Banking is now almost entirely computerised. Industrial espionage in most cases is a doddle. Most companies use fairly standard programming.'

Sergeant Knutter shook his head in disbelief. 'So you think the thief in this case was an amateur?'

★   ★   ★

'One of the old school, I'd say, caught up in the game mentality — of the Cambridge school perhaps — way behind the times.'

The detective sergeant looked at him doubtfully. 'It sounds like fiction to me. Could your wife do that?'

'Do what?'

'Crack a computer network.'

Mark shook his head. 'No. She, dear girl, is but a humble programmer. It would take an expert, but I know somebody who could.'

'Well, well,' Sergeant Knutter resumed his laborious task. 'I always thought these computer systems were supposed to be foolproof.'

Mark leaned forward again and whispered mischievously, 'Only a fool would think so.'

# 21

'Have you any news of Louise?' Edward Kelsey asked anxiously as he ushered Mark into his house.

'No. Have you?'

'Not a word.'

'You've not heard from Mrs. Breedon?' Mr. Kelsey looked startled. 'From her?'

'Of her then.'

'I went to find out when the funeral was to be. She's been a life-long member of our chapel so we'd like a proper memorial service.'

'When is it to be?'

Mr. Kelsey sighed. 'The police won't release the body.'

Mark gave a smirk of satisfaction. 'I'm not surprised. She's not dead.'

Kelsey stared at him. 'They said there would be a delay because of the inquest. Are you sure?'

'No,' Mark admitted. 'It's just a hunch. The only thing missing from her house was the picture of Rosa Luxemburg on the dresser.'

Mr. Kelsey nodded. 'I know the one. She was very proud of it. She was a bit of a romantic revolutionary in her youth. Fortunately not a bit practical when it came to politics. Some of her ideas were — well . . . '

'Crackpot?'

Mr. Kelsey grinned. 'To be honest, yes.'

'But she cherished that photograph?'

'Indeed, yes. She was never parted from it to my knowledge.'

Mark waved his hand triumphantly. 'Not something a thief would take is it? Ergo, she must have taken it herself.'

Mr. Kelsey sat on the sofa and scratched his head. He was very perplexed. 'Well, I hope you're right of course,' he said, 'but why would the police . . . ?' He shook his head in bewilderment. 'I wish I knew what this is all about.'

Mark sat opposite him on the edge of his seat so he could lean forward and said earnestly, 'Can I trust you?'

Something in his tone caught Kelsey's

attention. 'Of course you can,' he said sharply.

Mark pulled a face. 'Well, I'm going to,' he decided. 'I have to anyway. There's no one else. What's it all about? Well I can tell you this much. Lou has, or had, in her possession a stolen computer program.'

'Is it valuable?' asked Kelsey vaguely, feeling somewhat out of his depth.

'I'll say,' retorted Mark tersely. 'It contains details of a guided missile system being developed by the government. You can see why someone is after it.'

Mr. Kelsey looked shocked. 'I can't,' he said bluntly. 'How dreadful!' he exclaimed.

'Dreadful?' Mark failed to get his drift.

'That Louise should be mixed up in such a business.'

'I don't follow you.'

'Dreadful,' re-iterated Mr. Kelsey passionately, 'that we should pride ourselves on the sophistication of weapons of death, and that someone should desire them enough to kill for this kind of thing.'

Mark was amazed. 'What are you on about?'

Mr. Kelsey drooped like a sad old man. 'I'm sorry. I can't help myself. I've always been a pacifist. The very thought of war fills me with such horror. My father was gassed you know. Gassed in the trenches. He came home a broken man and he was only twenty-eight. I remember him well although I was very young. Twenty-eight and a broken man. He went away so tall and strong. Full of laughter. He spent the next ten years in a mental hospital. Committed suicide. Millions of young men wiped out in the first war. Thousands killed in the second, and now we're talking about whole cities, countries even being obliterated. I am whole-heartedly against the development of nuclear weapons. Disarmament has got to be the only way. If Louise took this thing to destroy it then I am with her all the way.'

Mark gazed at the old man. He spoke so fervently that if he had any doubts about his innocence they were dissipated. He shook his head wearily. 'You're naive,' he said bluntly.

Kelsey looked offended. 'That's my

fundamental belief. I can't help it. Such things should be done away with.'

'It can't be done.' Mark spoke unemotionally.

'Of course it can,' urged Kelsey warmly, 'with a will.'

Mark brushed his idealism aside with cold reason. 'Nonsense. You can't uninvent the atomic bomb — the bloody thing's been invented — anymore than you can uninvent gunpowder, although no doubt the world would be much better off if we stuck to slings and arrows. Every face of progress has its dark side. The greater the technology, the greater its capacity for misuse. The shadow of nuclear war is the price we pay for automatic washing machines, aeroplanes, space travel and, don't forget, the virtual eradication in half the world at least, of epidemic diseases which killed as indiscriminately as any bomb. It's easy to say 'let's go back' when you see something ahead that frightens you only history dosen't go back. It's a one-way street. Every generation has its enemies. They can't be got rid of by chucking the baby out with the bath-water.'

'You speak too glibly,' murmured Kelsey suppressing a delicate shudder, 'without understanding what it means to face these enemies.'

'You underestimate me,' replied Mark drily. 'War is terrible. Disease is terrible. Poverty is terrible. Man has always had to live with all three. If our new technology can lead to us cracking two out of the three I'd call that progress. There's a certain logic to human development but it's a binary logic — for every plus there is a minus, that's elementary mathematics. Progress must be balanced with caution because for every step forward — higher if you like — there is a greater danger that you might fall. You're a religious man. You must see the pattern of progress as part of a universal tapestry.'

'Yes, that's true,' Kelsey admitted.

'But what you don't see,' Mark admonished him, 'is that if it's woven with one continuous thread you can't unpick bits here and there without unravelling the whole damn thing.'

Kelsey looked doubtful. 'I take your

point,' he agreed, 'but I don't see any necessity to follow a path that will lead to destruction.'

Mark laughed. 'The world may blow up of its own accord. The planets may collide. The sun may go out like a candle in the wind. The future of the globe is a little beyond the scope of my intervention. All I know is there are some problems I can deal with. Technological developments present challenges and I like challenges.'

'You like danger, too,' observed Kelsey shrewdly.

Mark shook his head. 'I like adventure,' he amended. 'Intellectual adventure as much as physical. At the present I'm not in danger. It's Louise who concerns me. Can I use your phone? They may have a trace on mine.'

Mr. Kelsey nodded, although he still looked doubtful.

Mark picked up the phone and dialled a number, then waited for a reply.

'Sellingby?'

'Yes, speaking,' confirmed a smooth voice at the other end.

'This is McNamara. I want to arrange a trade.'

'What for what?' Sellingby sounded guarded.

'What for whom,' Mark corrected him. 'The tapes for my wife.'

'Your wife?'

'Unharmed. If you've touched a hair of her head . . . ' he hesitated. No point in losing his cool. ' . . . No deal. Right?'

Sellingby paused then asked, 'You've got the tapes?'

'I can keep my part of the contract. All I want is my wife back, a straight exchange, no complications.'

'No police?' queried Sellingby.

Mark snorted. 'I thought they were on your side.' There was silence as Sellingby seemed to be thinking the matter over. After a few moments had lapsed he came back silkily, 'All right, Mr. McNamara, you have a deal. We can meet you. There's an old cottage about three miles outside Ravenhill on the Derby Road. You can't miss it. Tumbledown old place, terribly picturesque. Moss growing in the rafters, bindweed round the door, that sort of thing. That do for you?'

'Sounds perfect,' retorted Mark grimly.

'Three o'clock suit you?' inquired Sellingby pleasantly as if he were making an ordinary appointment. 'Then we'll all be back in time for tea.'

'Three o'clock,' confirmed Mark. 'It's a pleasure doing business with you.'

'Not at all,' responded Sellingby politely. 'I'm sure the pleasure will be all ours.'

Mark put the receiver down. Mr. Kelsey watched him anxiously. 'Shouldn't you call the police?' he suggested tentatively.

Mark scowled. 'I can't trust the police.'

Mr. Kelsey's eyes widened. 'Surely you don't think . . . '

'I don't *know*,' Mark snapped, then recovering himself added evenly, 'I can't take any chances. I'm putting my faith in the Lord and his servant, namely you.' He jotted a name and number on a slip of paper and handed it over. 'If I'm not back by six o'clock ring this guy and tell him what's happened.'

'Who is he?' demanded Mr. Kelsey,

scrutinising the paper.

'The computer industry's answer to John Wayne,' said Mark humorously, 'at least, I hope he is. If he isn't he's going to be even more.'

'Even more what?'

'Short-staffed.'

★ ★ ★

Sellingby put down the telephone and looked thoughtful. 'That was McNamara,' he said to his companion. 'He wants to trade.'

'Trade?' Harrap looked up with a frown.

'He thinks we've got his wife.'

'But we haven't.'

Sellingby tutted impatiently. 'Don't be obtuse, Harrap. I know we haven't but it doesn't affect the situation materially. McNamara is prepared to meet us and hand over the tapes.' He rubbed his hands together smoothing the palms in deep satisfaction.

'Brilliant,' agreed Harrap sarcastically, 'and what happens when he finds we haven't got his wife?'

Sellingby raised his eyebrows superciliously. 'Don't anticipate difficulties, Harrap. You're so defeatist. We can cross that bridge when we come to it.'

# 22

Mark slipped on his leather jacket and tucked the tapes into his pocket. He patted them to make sure they were secure. Satisfied on this score he glanced around the room to see if there was anything else he needed. He went to the dresser drawer and took out an imaginary gun, mimed the act of polishing it and checking its sights, then shoved it into an imaginary shoulder holster. He practised drawing it rapidly and aiming it with two hands, legs splayed apart as he had seen American policemen do on the television. He replaced the gun in its imaginary holster and let his arms fall to his side. A fat lot of use that would be. All he had was his boy scout training and the indomitable instinct to survive of a born coward. He would be needing that.

He left the house and backed his car down the narrow street, turning it up an alley-way at the end so that he was headed across town for the Derby Road.

Sergeant Knutter watched Mark's car leave his house with a thoughtful expression on his face. Mark didn't see him, his concentration being all on the tricky manoeuvre he was performing. The policeman took note of the direction in which he was headed. He wondered where his own accomplices were at the moment. If the operation was going to plan he should be hearing from them very shortly. He took a handheld radio out of his pocket and tuned it in to the CB.

The Derby Road out of Ravenhill is a lonely stretch of trunk road that meanders up over the moor. Once the principal thoroughfare between Ravenhill and Derby it has given way to the new dual carriageway and tunnel that links up with a stretch of motorway joining Derby and Nottingham. This wider, faster road is now the preferred route for most drivers and the old A-road, now relegated to B-status, is virtually deserted by traffic, except in high summer when it is popular as a scenic route. On a fine day the view across the moor is breath-taking but in the afternoon, when Mark set out, a grey, damp mist swirled in the hollows and the high peaks were totally fog-bound. It was a day when the weather couldn't make up its mind whether to be wintry or wet. It was acutely depressing. The weight of the low clouds seemed to force an unwilling lethargy. Mark tried desperately to fight off the feeling. He needed all his wits about him. He sang 'Onward Christian Soldiers' as he went along, to fight off the sticky gloom that seemed to be penetrating the countryside like a creeping paralysis rendering every form of life inert. The bright tempo did seem to ward it off a bit, even though he couldn't remember all the words.

Three miles along the Derby Road he spotted the cottage. It was as Marcus Sellingby had described it, a tumbledown ruin. There was no other building in sight. On a fine day it might have looked picturesque with its rotting rafters and overgrown garden but as far as Mark could see it was merely derelict. The garden was surrounded by a tall thick hedge so the cottage was well shielded from prying eyes should anyone chance to pass. He could see no signs of life. A five-bar gate stood open alongside the garden and led into a field adjoining it. Mark turned his car into the rutted 'drive' and parked in the field. Cautiously he left the car and crept round to the front of the building. There was no other vehicle in sight. He concluded he was the first to arrive.

He pushed open the rotting front door and stepped under the low lintel into the cottage. Opposite him perched on an old kitchen table sat Sellingby — only Sellingby. Mark halted suspiciously.

'Good afternoon,' said Sellingby politely.

Mark hesitated then glanced round.

'Where's my wife?' he demanded, advancing purposefully.

'Look around you,' suggested Sellingby invitingly.

Mark spun round as the door slammed shut behind him to see Harrap standing in the shadows looking cold and frightened. 'What the — ?' he began but the words did not form themselves properly.

He felt a sharp, painful blow to the back of the head which was swiftly repeated. It came again as his knees began to buckle and he was just trying to patch together as a coherent thought the idea that he had walked into a trap when darkness closed round him.

He fell to the floor. Sellingby felt in his pockets and removed the tapes.

'What are we going to do with him?' asked Harrap. 'We can't leave him here.'

Sellingby toyed with the gun in his hand and pretended to aim it at Mark's head.

'No. I'm afraid Mr. McNamara has outlived his usefulness.'

'What about his wife?'

Sellingby shrugged. 'She's run away. She's of no importance to us now. As long as she keeps her head down we needn't worry about her. She never really knew anything, except where these were . . . ' he tapped the tapes against the tip of his nose. 'And we're about to relieve her of that responsibility.'

'De Wint should be here to take care of this,' Harrap complained, irritably poking his toe into Mark's inert body. 'This is his department.'

'I couldn't raise him. He seems to have disappeared,' Sellingby told him with his usual unflappable hauteur. 'We'll just have to deal with the matter ourselves.'

Harrap shuddered. 'I'm not going to kill him,' he said firmly. 'I draw the line at murder.'

Sellingby laughed at him. 'You make fine distinctions in your morality, old friend,' he observed softly. 'You sell weapons designed to kill thousands with appalling ferocity to pathological killers you know will not hesitate to use them against ignorant peasants, destroying their primitive villages, laying waste to the pathetic substance they scrape from their barren lands.'

'It's not like that,' objected Harrap.

Sellingby's mocking expression became more pronounced as the arch of his eyebrows lifted slightly. 'Isn't it? Allow me to remind you of the list of your customers . . . Uganda, Cambodia, Namibia, Angola, Chile, Argentina, Iraq, Iran, Israel, Lebanon . . . would you like

274

me to go on? The list is quite impressive. There's not a trouble spot in the world that dosen't have your trade-mark on it. You and Coca-cola. Quite an achievement.'

'I've never killed anyone,' insisted Harrap. 'I sell things that's all. What people do with them is their business. I'm just not going to be a party to murder, that's all.'

'You have no option,' retorted Sellingby sharply. 'You're already an accessory. What about Geoff Randall? You knew about him.'

'Not until after.'

'You knew.' Sellingby sniffed coldly to regain his superiority. He disliked showing emotion, even impatience seemed to crease the meticulous appearance he liked to put before the world. 'However, I shall not demand that you pull the trigger if you find it offensive.'

The little man hunched his shoulders petulantly. 'I just couldn't do it, that's all.'

Sellingby patted him indulgently. 'Then leave it to me.' He levelled the gun again at Mark's head.

'You're going to shoot him?' Harrap asked uneasily.

Sellingby allowed his hands to fall. 'I'm hardly going to inoculate him with this, am I?'

Harrap's face was creased with agony. 'What about the body?' 'The good inspector,' Sellingby lectured him patiently, 'has already told us what to do with the body — most obliging of him I'd say. If we dispose of it in one of the bogs on the moor the chances are it will never be found. If you look at that ordnance survey map on the table — excellent things ordnance survey maps, jewels of the H.M.S.O. — you will see that X marks the spot.'

'What spot?'

'A hundred yards behind this cottage is a patch of ground marked with little grassy symbols and for those, like you, who can't even comprehend that piece of simplicity, it says in beautiful italics 'Bog'.'

Harrap went over to inspect the map. Sellingby waited until he was satisfied then he gave his attention to Mark once more.

'He won't be heavy.' he remarked speculatively. 'He's tall but skinny. We should be able to manage him quite easily between us.'

'Are you going to do it in here?' asked Harrap uneasily.

Sellingby raised the gun again and took careful aim. 'You needn't look,' he said.

Harrap turned away and gasped.

'I shouldn't do that, if I were you, sir,' said Sergeant Knutter pleasantly.

Sellingby spun round. The hefty bulk of the policeman was blocking the rear entrance, where the door had all but rotted away. Sellingby's startled eyes went first to Knutter's impassive face then to the squat automatic held in his huge fist.

'Drop the weapon, please, sir' recommended Knutter placidly. 'Throw it into the corner behind you if you don't mind.'

Sellingby's face showed he knew the game was up. He was a sporting loser. He tossed the pistol into the dark area behind him where it clattered in among the rubble.

Sergeant Knutter looked down at Mark's tumbled body.

'He's not dead,' put in Harrap hastily, 'just unconscious.' 'Just as well, sir,' was Knutter's only comment.

He remained apparently immovably blocked in the doorway. Sellingby recovered a little of his poise and went to sit on the table. He took the map from Harrap and instinctively folding it neatly placed it squarely on his lap. Harrap stood beside him, head bowed like a naughty boy. He seemed to be silently crying.

'Chin up,' said Sellingby in the kindly tones of an elder perfect, 'Eight years max. With time off for good behaviour we'll be out in three. Isn't that so, Sergeant?'

'For conspiracy and attempted murder? Eighteen months I shouldn't wonder,' was the policeman's dry response.

'Exactly. They don't keep you in longer than they have to these days. It's like the hospitals. They need the beds.'

Harrap stifled a sob. 'What's my wife going to say?'

Sellingby could not answer this so he went on keeping his own upper lip decently rigid and ignored his distraught companion. 'I dare say they'll freeze our pensions. Mine's index-linked of course. Jolly good job under the circs,' he went on chattily. 'There's one question I must ask, of course. I believe its customary in this sort of situation and I'm a great one for tradition. First of all I suppose you want to know why I did it — ex-public schoolboy, pillar of the establishment and all that.'

'Money,' suggested Knutter frankly.

Sellingby was delighted. 'Money. Exactly. Well done, sergeant. I'm glad to see you know a good motive when you see one. None of this airy-fairy sociological stuff — no latent homosexuality you see? No desire to revenge myself against the emasculating bureaucracy that has controlled my life for the past — how many is it now — thirty-one years. Just money pure and simple. Harrap's the same. It's his life's ambition you know to make a dishonest fortune. Pity. We nearly succeeded.'

'What was your question, sir?' inquired the policeman without curiosity.

'Oh, yes,' Sellingby returned to his

original train of thought. 'How did you know where to find us?'

At this Sergeant Knutter, who had been responding to Sellingby's bravura performance by maintaining his own brand of stoicism could not prevent his features from spreading into a broad grin.

'As to that, sir,' he said lightly, 'I always believe the simplest methods are best. A couple of my lads have been following you.'

Outside two boys, one ginger-haired, one dark sat on the five-bar gate watching the road and waited for the police cars to arrive.

\* \* \*

As the police cars pulled into Shady Lane a crowd of people came out on to the steps of the station. Mark recognised Rufford among them at once. His sheer size gave him dominance over the rest. Beside him Edward Kelsey looked dwarfed. He appeared worried but his features relaxed into an expression of relief when he saw Mark in the second car and he beckoned to someone behind him. The car drew up at the kerb and Mark climbed out still feeling a little unsteady on his feet. As he looked up he saw Lou frantically pushing her way through the group. She clattered down the steps and ran towards him. A few yards away she stopped and said hesitantly, 'God, you look awful!'

He couldn't help himself. The words just slipped out. 'And where the hell have you been!'

His righteous indignation made her burst out laughing and she ran and threw her arms round him. 'You'll never guess,' she whispered in his ear, but by that time he'd lost interest.

He signed the statement where Inspector Williams had pointed with his finger and pushed the sheet across the desk.

'That it?'

'That's about the lot. Thanks for your co-operation and all that. You might have told us you were a secret agent.'

Mark laughed. 'I'm a software designer not a spy.' Inspector Williams gave him a funny look. 'Sounds like a funny set-up to me. Computer investigation is a new one on me. Ravenhill hasn't come to terms with the pocket calculator yet.'

'Systems analysis,' Mark corrected him. 'That covers a multitude of sins. You could say we were a civilian off-shoot of the Fraud Squad. Being freelance gives us a bit more latitude. Thanks for looking after Lou for me.'

Mark pocketed his pen. Inspector Williams waved away his gratitude modestly. 'Sorry we couldn't let you in on what we were doing but I had to be sure. One murder on my patch is enough. We nearly lost you though. If it hadn't been for Sergeant Knutter and his private army we would've done.'

'Those kids deserve a medal,' Mark said wryly. Even now he didn't care to reflect on how close it had been.

Inspector Williams agreed. 'I think we can arrange something. At the moment we've promised them a tour of the station and a trip out with one of the patrol cars. They're right chuffed with that. You're going back to London, are you?'

Mark nodded. 'In a day or two. I've got

an article to deliver to the paper, remember.'

Williams looked surprised. 'I thought the reporter's job was just a cover?'

Mark looked offended. 'Oh, no. I get paid for that, too.'

The policeman whistled enviously. 'Some people,' he said, 'have it made. What then?'

'Brussels,' Mark informed him. 'The European Agricultural Subsidies and their effect on the balance of National Economies.'

Inspector Williams grimaced. 'Sounds exciting.'

Mark reached for the door but before he went out he said with the ghost of a smile, 'Well you never can tell, can you?'

## THE END

We do hope that you have enjoyed reading this large print book.

Did you know that all of our titles are available for purchase?

We publish a wide range of high quality large print books including:
**Romances, Mysteries, Classics**
**General Fiction**
**Non Fiction and Westerns**

Special interest titles available in large print are:
**The Little Oxford Dictionary**
**Music Book, Song Book**
**Hymn Book, Service Book**

Also available from us courtesy of Oxford University Press:
**Young Readers' Dictionary**
**(large print edition)**
**Young Readers' Thesaurus**
**(large print edition)**

For further information or a free brochure, please contact us at:
**Ulverscroft Large Print Books Ltd.,**
**The Green, Bradgate Road, Anstey,**
**Leicester, LE7 7FU, England.**
**Tel:** (00 44) **0116 236 4325**
**Fax:** (00 44) **0116 234 0205**

# SEA VENGEANCE

## Robert Charles

Chief Officer John Steele was disillu-sioned with his ship; the *Shantung* was the slowest old tramp on the China Seas, and her Captain was another fading relic. The *Shantung* sailed from Saigon, the port of war-torn Vietnam, and was promptly hi-jacked by the Viet Cong. John Steele, helped by the lovely but unpredictable Evelyn Ryan, gave them a much tougher fight than they had expected, but it was Captain Butcher who exacted a final, terrible vengeance.

# THE CALIGARI COMPLEX

## Basil Copper

Mike Faraday, the laconic L.A. private investigator, is called in when macabre happenings threaten the Martin-Hannaway Corporation. Fires, accidents and sudden death are involved; one of the partners, James Hannaway, inexplicably fell off a monster crane. Mike is soon entangled in a web of murder, treachery and deceit and through it all a sinister figure flits; something out of a nightmare. Who is hiding beneath the mask of Cesare, the somnambulist? Mike has a tough time finding out.

# MIX ME A MURDER

## Leo Grex

A drugged girl, a crook with a secret, a doctor with a dubious past, and murder during a shooting affray — described as a 'duel' by the Press — become part of a developing mystery in which a concealed denouement is unravelled only when the last danger threatens. Even then, the drama becomes a race against time and death when Detective Chief Superintendent Gary Bull insists on playing his key role of hostage to danger.

# DEAD END IN MAYFAIR

## Leonard Gribble

In another Yard case for Commander Anthony Slade, there is blackmail at London's latest night spot. Ruth Graham, a journalist, and Stephen Blaine, a blackmail victim, pit their wits against unusual odds when sudden violence erupts. Then Slade has to direct the 'Met' in a gruelling bout of police work, which involves a drugs gang and a titled master-mind who has developed blackmail into a lucrative practice. The climax to the case is both startling and brutal.

# HIRE ME A HEARSE

## Piers Marlowe

Whenever Wilma Haven decided to be wayward, she insisted that she was seen to be wayward. So perhaps she was merely being consistent when she hired a hearse before committing suicide, then proceeded to take her time over the act in a very public place. However, Wilma died not from her own act, but by the murderous intent of an unsuspected killer, and Superintendent Frank Drury of Scotland Yard becomes embroiled in his most challenging case ever.